THE NOTHING to see HERE HOTEL

YOU ain't SEEN NOTHING YETI!

For Rosemary Sandberg,
Agent Extraordinaire!
SB

For Leonardo Charles Toime, Welcome to the world and The Nothing To See Here Hotel! SL X

First published in Great Britain in 2019 by Simon & Schuster UK Ltd
A CBS COMPANY

1 3 5 7 9 10 8 6 4 2

Simon & Schuster UK Ltd
1st Floor, 222 Gray's Inn Road
London
WC1X 8HB

www.simonandschuster.co.uk
www.simonandschuster.com.au
www.simonandschuster.co.in

Simon & Schuster Australia, Sydney
Simon & Schuster India, New Delhi

A CIP catalogue record for this book is available from the British Library.

PB ISBN: 978-1-4711-6385-2
eBook ISBN: 978-1-4711-6386-9

Printed and bound by CPI Group (UK) Ltd, Croydon, CR0 4YY

Simon & Schuster UK Ltd are committed to sourcing paper that is made from wood grown in sustainable forests and support the Forest Stewardship Council, the leading international forest certification organisation. Our books displaying the FSC logo are printed on FSC certified paper.

THE NOTHING to see HERE HOTEL

YOU ain't SEEN NOTHING YETI!

STEVEN BUTLER

ILLUSTRATED BY STEVEN LENTON

SIMON & SCHUSTER

You are viewing user reviews for The Nothing To See Here Hotel, Brighton

The Nothing To See Here Hotel

NB. Everyone is welcome at The Nothing to See Here Hotel (except humans... NEVER HUMANS!)

1,079 Reviews #1 of 150 Hotels in Brighton

Brighton Seafront UK BN1 1NTSH 00 11 2 334 4556 E-mail hotel

Francesca Simon

Reviewed 2 days ago

'A rip-roaring, swashbuckling, amazerous magical adventure. Comedy gold.'

Jeremy Strong

Reviewed 13 days ago

'A splundishly swashbungling tale of trolls, goblins and other bonejangling creatures. Put on your wellies and plunge into the strangest hotel you will ever encounter This is a hotel I hope I never find! Wonderfully, disgustingly funny.'

Cressida Cowell

Reviewed 29 days ago

'Hilariously funny and inventive, and I love the extraordinary creatures and the one thirty-sixth troll protagonist...'

You are viewing user reviews for The Nothing To See Here Hotel, Brighton

The Nothing To See Here Hotel

NB. Everyone is welcome at The Nothing to See Here Hotel (except humans... NEVER HUMANS!)

1,079 Reviews #1 of 150 Hotels in Brighton

Brighton Seafront UK BN1 1NTSH 00 11 2 334 4556 E-mail hotel

Reviewed 33 days ago

Liz Pichon

'This hotel gets five slimey stars from me...'

Reviewed 54 days ago

Jacqueline Wilson

'A magical hotel, known for its exclusive unique clientele. The chef is to be congratulated for inventing Bizarre Cuisine. All staff very friendly, but avoid the Manager (especially if you're wearing a cat-suit).'

Reviewed 75 days ago

Kaye Umansky

'What a fun hotel! Book me in immediately!'

WELCOME TO

WELCOME TO

THE NOTHING to see HERE HOTEL

WELCOME TO

THE NOTHING to see HERE HOTEL

THE NOTHING TO
SEE HERE HOTEL
Brighton S...

Dear ....

You have been specially selected for early booking at **The Nothing to See Here Hotel** on **February 22nd 2018**.

Are you are in need of a relaxing getaway or somewhere to escape the daily grind of lair lurking, bridge bothering or humdrum haunts? **The Nothing to See Here Hotel** is the place for you. We take honkhumptious pride in being the best secret holiday destination for magical creatures in the whole of England.

...ther it's soaking your scales in our pool, sampling the toothsome ...pider-cook extraordinaire, Nancy (her porcupaties ...) reading up on a curse or two ... we

Regurgita
Glump

Grottle
Glump

Rozomastrus
Bracegirdle

Grizhilda
Glump

Alfus
Chaff

Limina
Lightfoot

Lylifa
Glump

Crumpetra
Glump

Stodger
Banister

Rani
Roy

Frankie
Banister

Abraham Banister

Zennifer Glump

Ignotius Glump

Tussely Banister

Blundus Glump

Festus McGurk

Bombastis Banister

Bargeous Banister

Markle Banister

The Banister Family Tree

A RIGHT PICKLE!

'FRANKIE!'

I jolted awake with a yelp, flailing my arms about like an upturned tortoise. The scream was so loud it echoed round my bedroom and knocked my framed portrait of Great-Great-Great-Grandad Abraham off the wall.

'FRANKIE, COME QUICK!'

Sitting up in bed, I rubbed the sleep from my groggy eyes and glanced about, not sure if I was dreaming.

I'd been up late last night, helping Mum with an incident in the garden. Lady Leonora Grey, one of our ghost guests, had got so excited about winning a game of croquet that she'd accidentally exploded ectoplasm all over a family of hobyahs enjoying an evening outside. It was slime central! The Lawn was furious …

Hoggit, my pet pygmy soot-dragon, whimpered at me from the fireplace. All the yelling had made the orange glow between his scales turn to a pale grey, and he puffed out a chain of tiny smoke rings … a sure sign he was feeling nervous.

'FRANKIE! IT'S URGENT!'

It was Nancy, our hotel cook, speaking to me through the yell-a-phone, a trumpet-shaped contraption sticking out of the wall just above my head. The hotel is so big that we have a yell-a-phone in nearly every room so we can talk to each other wherever we are.

I stayed silent for a minute, deciding whether to pretend I hadn't heard her. Normally, if Mum, Dad or Nancy called me on the yell-a-phone in the morning, it was because they wanted me to help out with MEGA-BORING chores around the hotel, and I wasn't about to do that. I'm not noggin-bonked after all!

'ANSWER ME, DEAR, PLEASE!'

I pricked up my pointy ears. Nancy's voice sounded high-pitched and panicked.

'WE'RE IN A RIGHT PICKLE!'

'A RIGHT PICKLE!?' I gasped, then threw back the blankets and jumped out of bed. If you'd spent any time at all in our hotel, you'd know that 'a right pickle' could mean any sort of disaster!

We'd had a 'right pickle' just last week when a Madagascan muskrumple smashed through the kitchen wall and demolished half the cupboards after he found out we'd run out of bread rolls to go with the seagull-snot soup!

OH! Hang on a second! I've just realised that if you haven't read any of my books before, you're probably wrinkling up your forehead and saying, 'WHAT ON EARTH IS HE TALKING ABOUT?'

Well, don't panic! There are definitely one or two things you need to know before we carry on, but it'll only take me a moment. I'm super good at telling stories. Madam McCreedie, one of our banshee guests, said so … and banshees are NEVER wrong.

I should probably start with an introduction. HELLO! My name is Frankie Banister and I live in the Nothing To See Here Hotel.

Ever been to stay here for your holidays?

Ha! Of course you haven't! It's the best holiday destination for magical creatures in the whole of the UK and we have a STRICTLY NO HUMANS rule.

Well … no humans unless you're married to a

magical, like my mum. She's completely human and my dad is what's known as a halfling, which makes me a quarterling, I suppose. Yep, I'm one thirty-sixth troll and proud of it.

Ever since my great-great-great-human-grandad, Abraham Banister, married my great-great-great-troll-granny, Regurgita Glump, about a hundred years ago, my family tree has been a proper muddle. It's full of trolls and humans, witches, bogrunts, puddle nymphs and just about every other type of magical creature you can think of. Brilliant, huh?

Let's not worry too much about all that family stuff now though. I'll fill you in on the details as we go, I promise, plus I've stuck a picture of my family tree at the beginning of this book for you to have a peek at.

Now, I know it all seems a bit impossible – I'm sure this sounds like a bunch of silly nonkumbumps – but I'm not even kidding. If you've read my first book, you'll know that Frankie Banister NEVER tells lies.

My name really IS Frankie Banister, I really DO

live with my mum and dad, Rani and Bargeous, in a hotel for magical creatures on Brighton's seafront, and Nancy the giant spider (ooops! I forgot to mention that part) had just ruined my sleep, warning me about a right pickle.

So, before you throw this book in the bin, shouting, 'I'M NOT READING THIS! FRANKIE BANISTER HAS POPPED HIS CLONKERS! THIS IS GOING TO BE THE WEIRDEST TALE EVER!', read on just a teensy bit more …

You'll be hooked in no time, I just know it.

'Nancy?' I barked

into the metal trumpet of the yell-a-phone. 'I'm here!'

'Ooooh! Frankie! I've been calling you for yonks and yonkers!'

'What's happened?' I shouted, suddenly feeling a queasy mix of excitement and fear bubble up in my tummy. 'A plague of gurnips? A Kraken in the swimming pool? A coachload of Stink Demons?'

'No, my dearie,' Nancy wailed. 'It's much, **MUCH** worse than that. Get down here as quick as you can! **IT'S RUINED! THE DAY'S RUINED!!!'**

I didn't need telling twice. I scooped Hoggit out of the fireplace, jumped into the armchair in the corner of my room, clicked the dial on its arm to the correct position and impatiently waited as it juddered down through my bedroom floor to the library below.

TROGMA-WHAT?!

It was obvious something was wrong as I reached the ground floor with a bump.

I'd only just clambered out of the chairlift when I heard the library wallpaper grumbling.

Yep! I told you our hotel was weird. It's our version of normal around here, I suppose.

Anyway … it doesn't take long for juicy news to spread when you're living in a magical hotel. The walls have ears – quite literally! Nothing in the whole world loves to gossip quite as much as our enchanted wallpaper does. It's covered in nattering clamshells and painted vines that blossom and wilt as the seasons change, and everyone knows that rumours travel quickest by vine. I swear – keeping a

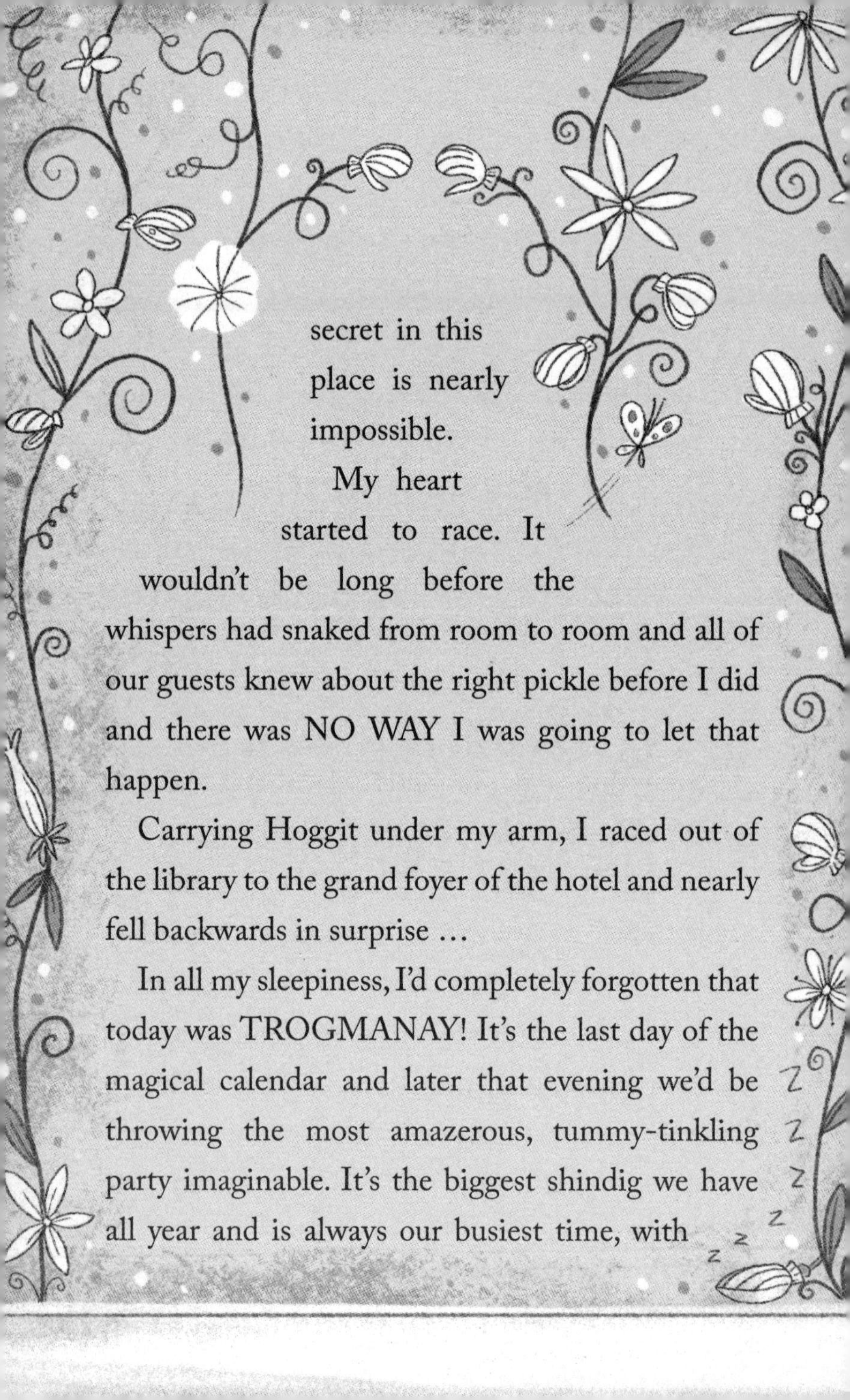

secret in this place is nearly impossible.

My heart started to race. It wouldn't be long before the whispers had snaked from room to room and all of our guests knew about the right pickle before I did and there was NO WAY I was going to let that happen.

Carrying Hoggit under my arm, I raced out of the library to the grand foyer of the hotel and nearly fell backwards in surprise …

In all my sleepiness, I'd completely forgotten that today was TROGMANAY! It's the last day of the magical calendar and later that evening we'd be throwing the most amazerous, tummy-tinkling party imaginable. It's the biggest shindig we have all year and is always our busiest time, with

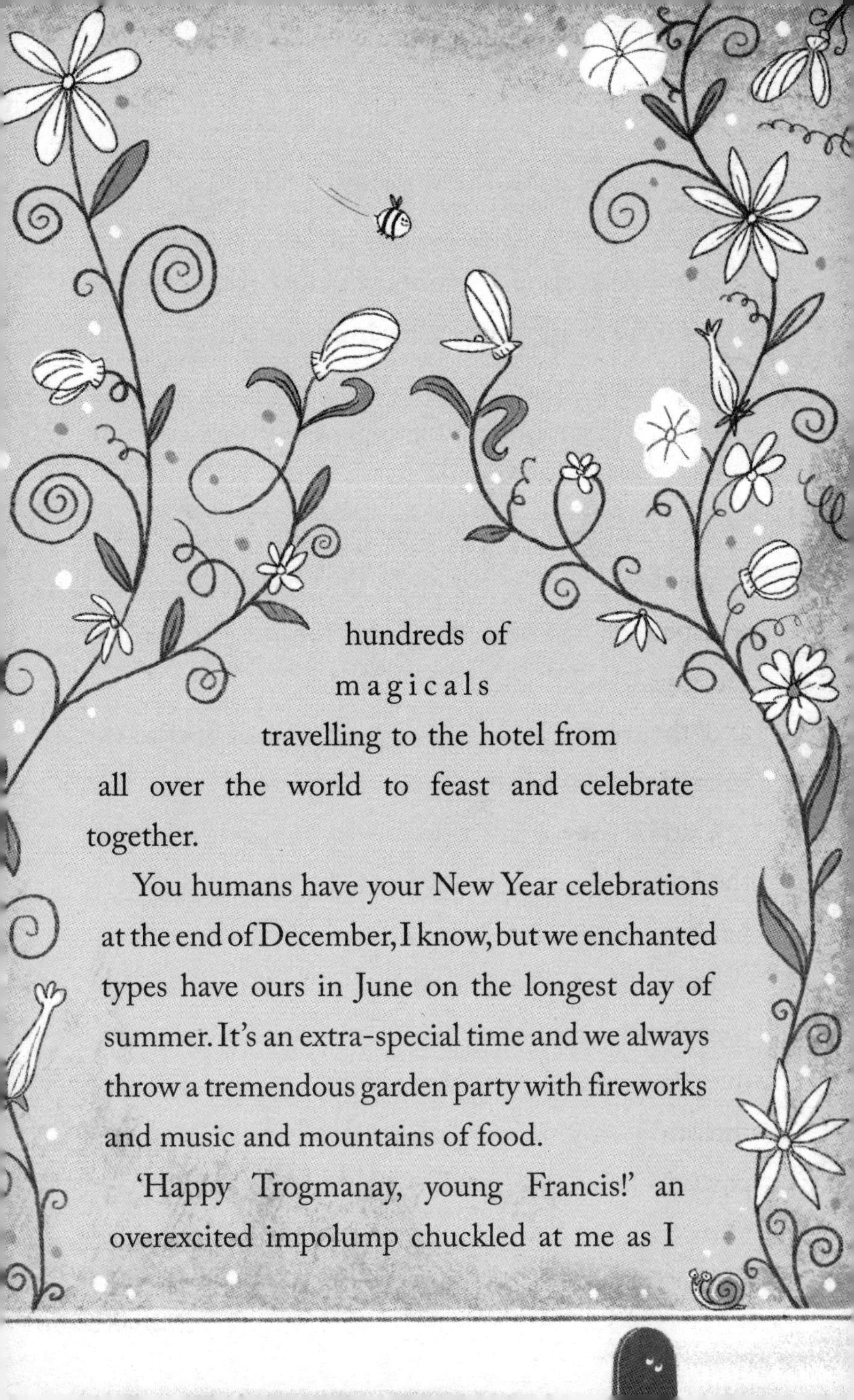

hundreds of magicals travelling to the hotel from all over the world to feast and celebrate together.

You humans have your New Year celebrations at the end of December, I know, but we enchanted types have ours in June on the longest day of summer. It's an extra-special time and we always throw a tremendous garden party with fireworks and music and mountains of food.

'Happy Trogmanay, young Francis!' an overexcited impolump chuckled at me as I stood gawping in the doorway. I HATE it when people call me Francis, but I smiled and nodded regardless as the impolump waddled away, carrying an armful of gifts, grinning from ear to ear. 'A jolly trolliday to you!'

I glanced around for a moment and almost forgot about finding Nancy as quickly as possible. Reception was already crowded and bustling with cheerful guests, waving and nattering, and everything had been decorated for our big summer celebration. It looked TERRIFIC!

Mr Croakum, the hotel gardener, had decked the chandeliers with bunches of bizarre flowers that changed colour from yellow, to blue, to purple, to pink, and there were enchanted garlands of bright orange marigolds all around the spiral staircase that wept a constant rainfall of petals down on the happy holidaymakers below.

Gladys Potts, the werepoodle, was howling her favourite trolliday songs from the first-floor balcony and Madam McCreedie was reading a book of Trogmanay ghost stories to a group of nervously giggling grumplings at the bottom of the stairs.

'That's not how I remember it,' Lady Leonora Grey scoffed, plucking a ghostly fan from the air and wafting herself with it when McCreedie got to an especially spooky part of her story. 'Do you, Norris?' She turned to where Wailing Norris, another of our ghost guests, had been floating, but he'd already screamed and run away.

'It'th all tho fethtive!' said one of the Molar Sisters (triplet tooth fairies called Dentina, Gingiva and Fluora) as the trio spun round the floor, performing a traditional celebration jig. They wobbled and shimmied about like three Trogmanay trifles, gnashing their rotten teeth merrily. 'Happy dayth indeed!'

I spotted Mum at the stone reception desk. She was busily checking a line of moss gremlins in for the weekend, and fussing at the same time about a vase of dead flowers Mr Croakum had left behind on the counter.

The hotel handyogre, Ooof, was next to Mum, holding a tray filled with glasses of fizzy trog-ma-grog cocktails.

'HELLO, FRANKIE!' Ooof yelled, waving a massive green arm and accidentally throwing the tray of drinks right across the room. It smashed through one of the windows next to the front door and vanished out of sight down the garden path. 'OOOPS!'

That was when Mum looked up and saw me.

'JOLLY TROLLIDAYS!' she beamed. 'Morning, sleepyhead! Look at you, still in your pyjamas.'

Mum always loves magical celebrations. I mean really, REALLY LOVES THEM! I think it's

because she's completely human so it all seems extra brilliant to her.

I headed round the fountain in the middle of the black and white tiled floor, reached the reception desk and was just about to open my mouth when—

'I'm so excited!' Mum said, clapping her hands. 'This Trogmanay is going to be the best one we've ever had … I can feel it!' She looked so happy that I wouldn't have been surprised if her head had floated off her shoulders.

'Mum, I—'

'I can't wait to see what Nancy's rustling up for our festive feast,' she said, practically giggling. 'I hope there's plenty of scrambled unicorn eggs.'

Nancy!!! I was wasting time. I had to go and find out about the RIGHT PICKLE…

Whatever had happened, it was obvious that Mum didn't know … and that was a good thing.

Mum would have thrown a serious wobbler if she knew we were in the middle of a yet another drama … especially on Trogmanay

'GROOOAAAARRR!' Hoggit wriggled

in my arms and blew out more little smoke rings. Mum spotted it immediately.

'What's wrong with Hoggit?'

'I … ummm … no … I … nothing.'

'Francis!' Mum's face fell into a frown. 'What's going on?'

'Nothing,' I said again, pulling my best happy face. I felt like my heart was about to play a tune on the inside of my ribs and give me away. 'Hoggit's just filled with Trogmanay cheer, aren't you, boy?'

Mum stared for a second. 'Something's wrong, I can te—'

'See you, Mum!' I shouted, far too loudly. 'Happy Trogmanay!' And, before she could say another word, I spun on my heels and raced out of reception.

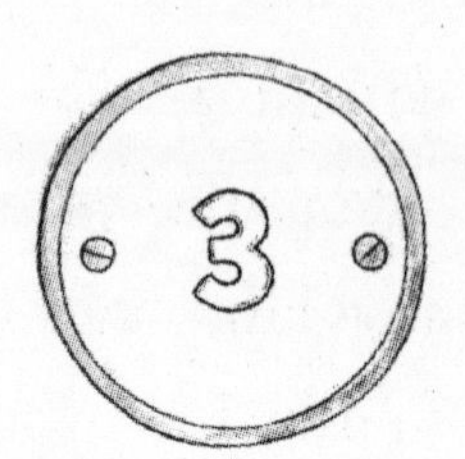

NANCY'S NEWS

I sprinted down the hallway, past the dining room and found a gaggle of potato-sized dust pooks jostling about outside the kitchen.

'Pickle, pickle, pickle,' they squeaked in unison, banging their tiny hands on the bottom of the closed door. 'Pickle, pickle, pickle!'

'Excuse me,' I said, stepping over them. News was spreading quicker than I had imagined!

'What's all this about a pickle?' Reginald Blink, the cyclops, called to me from further down the

hall. 'My bedroom walls are mumbling about it non-stop!'

'I don't know...' I said.

'Are we talking about the trouble kind, or the brown, squishy kind that goes with cheese? If it's the squishy kind, you can count me in!'

'Sorry ... I ... umm ...'

Turning the handle, I darted through the door only to find Dad sitting at the kitchen table with his head in his hands and Nancy standing in the middle of the room like a startled, eight-legged statue. She was clutching shopping bags in her four hands and there were more dotted about on the floor around her fluffy-slippered feet.

'What's happened?' I half-whispered, half-spat as I closed the door behind me and put Hoggit down on a pile of dishcloths.

'Oh, Frankie!' Nancy gasped, jumping with fright.

'What took you so long?' She dropped one of the bags with a loud CRASH of glass jars, then clutched a hand to her chest. 'For a second there I thought it might be your mother.'

'What on earth is going on?' I asked.

Dad lifted his face from his hands. He looked at me miserably, then glanced over at our giant spider-cook.

'Tell Frankie what you just told me,' he said to Nancy. 'Rani's going to be so upset. She LOVES TROGMANAY!'

'Oh, blunkers! Nancy said, putting down the rest of her shopping. 'I'll tell you, my wee lamb, but we'll need tea … definitely tea…'

I watched as she crossed the room to hang up her shawl by the conservatory door. There was a mirror on the wall next to the coat hooks and, despite the nervous gurgling in my stomach, I couldn't help but smile to myself when I spotted Nancy's reflection in it.

Instead of the giant Orkney Brittle-Back spider that we all see, a short human granny in a flowery housecoat stared back at her from the glass. It was an enchantment called a glimmer that Nancy used so she could go shopping in supermarkets without being spotted. It hadn't quite worn off yet, by the look of things.

Loads of magicals use spells like that and pass among you and your families on the street every day. I mean it! Next time you're out at the shops, keep a keen eye on people's shadows. That's the only thing that gives them away… You might be looking at an adorable little girl with pigtails and a spotty dress, but her shadow is that of an enormous tusk-billed plunktipuss!

'Well, I'd popped down to the seafront to the grocer's to get some mango chutney,' Nancy began. (This is probably a good time to tell you that most human food tastes disgusting to us, but magicals LOVE extra-thick and spicy mango chutney. They can't get enough of it to spread on their cuttlefish crumpets at Trogmanay!)

'And?' I said, itching to find out what happened next.

'But there was pandemonium EVERYWHERE!' she said, pouring hot water into a teapot.

'Pandemonium?' I asked. 'Why?'

'That's what I wondered too.' Nancy's eight eyes widened and I knew she was getting to the good bit. 'Everywhere I turned there were humans running about, frantically grabbing anything they could lay their hands on from the shelves of every shop. Och, it was madness.'

Nancy placed three mugs on the table and poured us each a steaming mug of shrimp-scale tea.

'I managed to swipe a newspaper from the magazine stand near the pier and it turns out there's an enormous freak blizzard heading this way. A huge, swirling snowstorm that's due to arrive here in England any time soon!'

'A blizzard ...' groaned Dad. 'I just can't believe it!'

'That's impossible!' I joined in. 'It's June!'

We all glanced over to the window at the brilliant sunshine outside. I could see that Dad had already set up the barbecue on the patio and Mrs Dunch, the very old and very wrinkly mermaid, was sunning herself in her starfish bikini at the top of the waterslide by the pool.

'Exactly!' said Nancy. 'According to the newspaper, human scientists are baffled! The storm came down from Asia and has crossed Europe, freezing everything in its path. Apparently the Eiffel Tower in Paris has been turned into a giant icicle!'

'Our summer celebration is going to be dreadful!' Dad whined. 'No one will ever visit us again. How can we have a proper Trogmanay Trolliday if it's like the North Pole outside?'

Suddenly I gasped as something Nancy had said just seconds ago sparked a memory in my brain.

'Hang on!' I said to her, feeling a tingle of excitement. 'What did you just say about the storm?'

'That the blizzard has baffled human scientists—'

'No, not that part!'

'That it's come all the way from Asia and across Europe?' said Nancy, squinting at me suspiciously.

'Yes, that!' I barked. 'THAT'S GREAT NEWS!'

'What is?' asked Dad as confusion spread across

his face like a rash.

'Are you all right, Frankie?' Nancy said, placing a hand on my forehead.

The two of them stared at me blankly for a moment, then Dad slowly realised what I was talking about.

'It can't be…' Dad glanced over at Nancy as a huge smile spread across his face.

Nancy giggled at Dad as she realised too.

'Do you really think so?' she said, clapping her hands.

'It has to be!' I almost yelled, slamming my mug down on the table with glee.

Now, before you get cross with me, shouting, 'I DON'T UNDERSTAND! WHAT ARE THEY ALL GRINNING AT AND TALKING ABOUT?!', I'll tell you.

Ready for a short and snappy history lesson?

Back when my dad was younger, his human urges kicked in and he got mega mopey and moany, the way all teenagers do … I've heard anyway.

So, he decided to go off travelling around the world to 'FIND HIMSELF', just like Great-Great-Great-Grandad Abraham used to do, and Dad ended up staying in a yeti village on the highest slopes of Mount Everest.

He tried yoga and dinging bells and burning herbs and fasting and feasting and chanting strange words and all that wafty-lofty stuff… He didn't 'find himself', but he DID find his BESTEST lifelong yeti friend, Orfis Kwinzi!

And, every so often, we get a visit from Orfis and his family, and any magical with half a brain knows yetis always travel at the centre of a stonking great magical blizzard, so nobody spots them…

'If it is the Kwinzis, we'll have to throw them an extra-special party,' said Nancy. 'What a lovely treat for Trogmanay!'

'OH, MY GOODNESS!' Dad suddenly shot up from the table and his face dropped from a smile to a look of complete and utter panic. 'What are we doing just sitting here? IT'S TROGMANAY!

WE'VE GOT A HOTEL FULL OF GUESTS CHECKING IN FOR THE SUMMER TROLLIDAY WEEKEND!' he blurted. 'THEY'RE ALL GOING TO GET SNOWED IN!'

He was right. If Orfis and his family were on their way to us, the blizzard they brought with them would be a whopper, freezing everything for miles around.

'AAAAGH!' With that, Dad ran out through the kitchen door, scattering dust pooks this way and that, like grubby little tennis balls, then sprinted off down the hallway, screeching, 'WE HAVE TO WARN YOUR MOTHER!'

NEW ARRIVALS

By the time I caught up with Dad, he was hurrying behind the stone counter in the reception hall.

I watched him attempt to tell Mum the news, but she was far too busy dealing with guests to listen.

In the short time I'd been in the kitchen, the enormous foyer had completely filled up with hordes of holidaymakers, ready for the Trogmanay weekend.

A line of boggarts, a Japanese dogu, some chirping stag-bunkles, an ancient pine dryad and a family of grime fairies had formed in front of Mum.

'We have a deluxe hutch freshly prepared for you all,' I heard Mum say as she checked in a family of rabbity hinkapoots. She smiled at them, still blissfully unaware that things were about to get very cold. 'Will you be wanting a wake-up carrot?'

Mum glanced over at me with a grin on her face, then gestured for me to help an elderly anemononk climb out of the open sea door in the middle of the spiral floor. The old thing was twitching his bright pink-and-orange feelers this way and that, grumbling to himself.

'Welcome to the Nothing To See Here Hotel,' I said, grabbing at his hand. He wrapped his jelly-like tentacles round my wrist and I tried my best not to grimace as the slimy sea creature slithered up over the edge of the deep well.

'Thank you kindly, young man,' the anemononk half-rasped, half-gurgled at me. 'Me suckers ain't what they used to be…' Then he gave a bubbling, sludgy laugh and slopped off in the direction of the reception counter.

'Frankie?'

I jumped with surprise as Dad put a hand on my shoulder. 'On second thoughts, don't mention anything about the storm,' he whispered. 'There's no point upsetting you-know-who if it turns out to be just a regular one. Sometimes human forecasters get these things wrong, so it might be nothing. Go to the window and keep an eye on things.'

Mum looked over and Dad smiled his best 'everything's fine' smile at her before hurrying back to help at the front desk.

Maybe Dad was right not to cause an unnecessary fuss. Mum loved celebrating the magical holidays SO much and it would be a shame to spoil it for her if we didn't need to. Plus, things had already been really strange at the Nothing To See Here Hotel lately.

Really, REALLY STRANGE!

Only six weeks ago, we'd all watched in horror as Prince Grogbah, the thieving heir to the throne of the Barrow Goblins, had been accidentally swallowed by Mrs Venus (Mr Croakum's giant, flowery, fly-trap wife). That was after the entire hotel had been stormed by goblin pirates and nearly wrecked in a swash-bungling battle!

HA! How's that for a crazy paragraph? But it's all true…

Mum had been on high alert ever since, making sure absolutely nothing went wrong for the Trogmanay Trolliday.

I walked over to the smashed window next to the front door and stared out at the horizon. So far, so sunny … or…

There, just above the line of the sea, was a big dark smudge of cloud against the bright blue sky.

It was impossible to tell if I was looking at an enchanted storm from this far away, but the more I watched it, the more I could see the clouds were growing and heading towards us. Whether it was a magical blizzard or not, it seemed certain the bad weather was going to reach Brighton.

So much for a sunny party outside. Dad was right that a freak snowstorm could cause a Trogmanay disaster, but if our yeti friends from across the globe were the reason for the storm then it would all be worth the cold! The guests might have a good grumble that their summer fun was ruined, but the idea of celebrating the trolliday with snowball fights and sledging gave me goosebumps with excitement.

I was just about to get Dad's attention and update him about the dark smudge on the horizon when the sky-door mechanism jolted into action, and the black and white rings on the floor started spinning in different directions beneath our feet.

'Incoming!' Mum yelled as I rattled past her, trying to keep my balance while dodging the elderly anemanonk at the same time.

'Ere what's going on?' the old sea creature gurgled, frantically wrapping his feelers around a hat-stand for dear life. 'It's a whirlpool!'

'Oooh, lummy!' The Molar Sisters called from the third floor balcony. 'I hope it'th thomeone dentithty!'

'Or edible!' Madam McCreedie joined in from the entrance to the library.

A shaft of sunlight suddenly streamed down through the centre of the spiral staircase as the door slid away, ten floors up, and I squinted to see who was arriving.

'Who could this be?' Dad said, looking mildly panicked as he jogged against the turning floor next to me. 'Yetis can't fly, so it certainly isn't them.'

MAUDLIN MALONEY DROPS IN

'STEADY!' a cracked voice suddenly shrieked as a dark, square shape came tumbling down through the hole in the ceiling. **'STEADY AS SHE GOES!'**

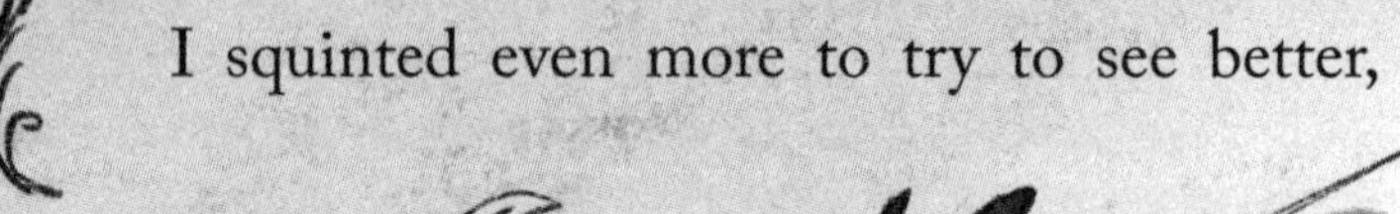

I squinted even more to try to see better,

then instantly forgot about yeti visitors and Trogmanay feasts as a feathery house came hurtling into view.

'BRACE YOURSELVES, GIRLS!' the voice yelled.

I've said squillions of times before that I really DO see crazy things every single day, but this was a shock even for me. I'd never seen anything like it!

The house plummeted towards us, spinning and

ricocheting off the staircase landings with dreadful crunches and flurries of feathers.

'PULL UP!' the shrill voice started to howl from inside the falling object. 'Pull up, ladies, or we'll be splattered, so we will!'

My heart jumped into my throat and I grimaced, trying to look away. Any second now, the wooden shack would shatter against the floor and…

Just as we all started screeching in unison, thinking the queue of impatient guests at reception were about to be squished flatter than Nancy's badger-milk pancakes, the house came to a wobbly stop in mid-air above our heads.

For a second there was only a stupefied silence, then everybody screamed and bolted to safety, except for one of the boggarts, who wheezed a startled croak at his wife and children and promptly fainted.

As the sky door creaked back into place above us, I finally got a good look at the unidentified falling object and my mouth drooped silently open at the bizarre sight. It wasn't a feathery house at all.

Suspended in the air above reception was a caravan, about a quarter of the size of the type a human would live in. It looked like the pictures you see in books, with brightly patterned walls and a few squat chimneys poking out through a rounded roof tiled in rusted coins!

Where most caravans have a horse or donkey at the front to pull them along, this one had several ropes sticking out of its windows, each clutched in the claws of a frantically flapping chicken. There must have been twenty of them!

The poor things were half-bald and looked like they were going to pass out or let go at any moment.

'BWARK!' one of them ca-cawed, beating its wings so hard it looked like they might drop off.

'B-KAWK!' called another as an egg splatted on the foyer floor … and then another … and another.

'What's that, ladies?' The front door of the caravan burst open and one of the most grizzled faces I'd ever seen leaned out. 'Would you look at that … safely on dry land! We made it!'

Everybody gasped and a ripple of fearful mumbling went round the room. It was a leprechaun.

Now, if there's one magical creature that you humans have got so, so, SO wrong in stories over the centuries, it's these Irish fairies.

In really-real life, leprechauns aren't anything like the little men in green suits you read about or see on TV.

NOT EVEN CLOSE!

They are only ever female, for instance, and they're never jolly or found skipping about at the end of a rainbow, and their magic charms are mostly extremely unlucky.

'Um…' Dad slowly raised a hand and waved to catch her attention. 'W-welcome?'

The leprechaun jolted with surprise when she spotted our faces goggling up at her.

'Oh, would you look at you all,' she said, eyeing the crowd and the drop to the floor. She stared for a long time with the expression of someone who'd swallowed a wasps' nest, then rapped on the ceiling above her. 'We didn't quite make it, ladies …

LOWER!'

The exhausted chickens slowed their crazed flapping and the caravan juddered downwards until it hit the black and white tiles with a BUMP, narrowly missing the unconscious boggart.

'Is this the place?' the little creature grunted, stepping out onto the floor.

I'd never seen a leprechaun before (except in Great-Great-Great-Grandad Abraham's dusty old books), but I'd been warned about them hundreds of times. They were very tricksy and often brought terrible bad luck with them, wherever they went.

'I said, is this the place?' she asked again. 'The Nothing To Something Something Hotel?'

Nobody spoke. All we could do was gawp at the strange, stumpy creature with a face like hammered meat and tangled grey dreadlocks that snaked about her shoulders and back like mouldy rags. Both arms were covered in twisty blue tattoos and her gnarled fingers (she was missing a few) were stacked with row upon row of gold rings.

'What are those?' one of the boggart children

asked, pointing to a leathery clutch of shrunken heads hanging from the leprechaun's belt. The boggart mother quickly shushed her son and pulled him away.

'Ooooh, these are me most precious, most dark and dooky unlucky charms,' the leprechaun said with a leer. 'Would you like one?'

Nobody answered.

'This one here,' the ancient bad luck fairy hissed, clutching at a particularly gruesome-looking lump of a head, 'was my Aunt Influenza. She had it comin', so she did. The noggin-knocker forgot to put sugar in me cocoa.'

Still nobody made a peep.

'What's the matter with you all?' she barked as everyone took a step backwards. 'Have your tongues been swiped by rattle-snitches?'

Mum suddenly came to her senses and bounded out from behind the stone counter, beaming her 'customer service' smile.

'I do apologise,' she said, reaching out to shake the leprechaun's hand, then instantly yanking

hers away again. Anyone with even a shred of intelligence knows never to touch the unluckiest fairy in the magical world. 'You just took us by surprise … that's all.'

'Surprise?'

'Mmm-hmmm.' Mum gave a painful smile.

'Haven't you ever seen a lepre-caravan flown by chickens before?'

'I didn't think chickens could fly!' The words came out of my mouth before I was able to stop them.

'Oh?' The grizzled old thing turned and scowled at me. For a moment I felt sure I'd made her angry, but then her forehead creased in thought.

'Well, that explains the bumpy ride.' She cackled with laughter. 'Ain't that right, girls?'

The chickens cooed and clucked a weary

response, already nestling in to roost on the caravan roof.

'Welcome to the Nothing To See Here Hotel! Are you here for the trolliday weekend, Madam?' asked Dad, joining Mum at her side, but keeping a safe distance from our new guest.

'Madam?' The leprechaun scoffed. 'What nonsense! Maloney's the name.' She grinned, showing a mouthful of teeth so wonky and dirty they looked like gravestones. 'Maudlin Maloney.'

'Welcome, Miss Maloney,' Mum said. 'Can we interest you in a room? We're very busy, but I'm sure we can squeeze you in somewhere…'

'What would I be wantin' a room for when I've got me own lepre-caravan parked right in your reception?' Maudlin interrupted. 'Here'll do just fine, methinks.'

Mum looked like she'd just been slapped round the face.

'And I don't care about all that Trogmanay twaddle and fancyish foolery! Spittle-trump, if you ask me!' Miss Maloney continued. 'I just want to get me some sun. **GLORIOUS, RUMP-ROASTING SUNSHINE!** It's all me cold and cankery heart desires, don't you know? I've been dreamin' of warmin' me wumplets and cosyin' me carbuncles for yonkers now. These tired old bones are half-rotten with the chill of Tipperary torrents. I can't take any more cold. I'll bust me boogles if I have to spend one more dooky day a-shiverin'!'

Dad shot me a worried look, then glanced at the windows, searching for signs of snow.

'You've come to the right place,' Mum said, smiling. 'You'll love our mud spa, and the pool deck is drenched in sunlight all day long.'

'Music to me papery ears!'

'We also have lots of … ummm … blankets,' Dad stammered.

The old leprechaun fixed him with her icy stare

and scowled.

'Blankets?' she hissed. 'Why would I be wantin' blankets? Who the blunkers are you?'

'Banister,' said Dad, looking like he might burst into tears. 'Bargeous Banister.'

'Any relation to Abraham Banister?'

'Yes, actually,' Dad said. 'Abraham was my great-great-grandfather.'

Dad gestured up to the framed portrait of Grandad Abraham that hung above reception.

'Oh, there he is, the ratsome old dog.' Maudlin chuckled. 'I knew Old Abe well in me earlier years … and his son there.'

'Pardon?' I asked, forgetting my nervousness and taking a few steps closer.

'Hmmm?' Miss Maloney grunted.

'Did you say "son"?'

I glanced up at the portrait, which was identical to the one in my room. In the picture, Abraham was standing at the centre of a jungle clearing with a pale, dark-haired boy. I'd asked a squillion times before who the child was, but no one could ever tell me … not even Great-Great-Great-Granny Regurgita.

'That's right. I knew old Abe and his son,' Maudlin said.

'Abe and Regurgita didn't have a son,' said Dad. He looked about as confused as I felt.

'They only have two daughters. There's

Grottle Glump, who lives in Mexico on her foozle farm these days, and then there's Zennifer Glump.' He pointed to the water witch in the middle of the fountain.

Oh, I think I forgot to mention that the statue in our reception was once my great-great-aunt Zennifer.

Yep! I told you my family were weird…

Years before I was born, Zennifer got into an argument with a Gorgon guest about the right shampoo for glossy snake scales. Needless to say the Gorgon won and Aunt Zennifer has been a stone art installation ever since.

'Oh, ignore me,' Maudlin said, waving a hand back and forth like she was swatting flies. 'Me clunkered old memory is dusty and dog-eared – it must be playin' tricks. Anyway, Mr Banister, you were sayin'?'

'Ah … umm, yes … I manage the hotel along with my wife, Rani, and our son,' said Dad. He nodded in my direction and Miss Maloney laid her cold stare on me again.

'Aha! So the chatterish quarterling belongs to you?'

'H-hello,' I stammered, wondering how she knew I was a quarterling. Something about this gristly old grunion made me even more nervous than Great-Great-Great-Granny Regurgita did. 'My name is—'

'Don't tell me,' she barked, holding up a three-fingered hand. She stepped close and sniffed the air between us. 'You are Francis Gringus Banister.'

I gasped in surprise and could feel my cheeks burning. How did she know my middle name? It's even worse than Francis and I absolutely hate it.

When naming me, Mum and Dad thought it would be a great idea to go with something super traditional, so they took inspiration from a distant relative, Gringus the Great, a flatulence-wump who once split a mountain in half with the power of his … well, never mind. It's so awful and I've never shared that fact with another living soul. It's my deepest, darkest secret and Mum and Dad are sworn to silence.

'Haha!' she cooed, when she saw the expression on my face. 'Manky old Maloney knows everythin'.' She tapped a crooked finger against the side of her nose, then winked and turned away.

'Gringuth!' the molar sisters shouted down from the balcony. 'What a gorgeouth name!'

'That's my second cousin's name,' the pine dryad called out from the crowd. 'And come to think of it … that's my name too!'

I was so embarrassed! This ancient bad-luck fairy was more powerful than I'd imagined.

I hope the blizzard arrives and ruins your summer trip, you miserable goat! I thought to myself.

'As I was sayin', Mr Banister, before I got rudely interrupted with all this talk of families,' Maudlin Maloney said to Dad, 'you can keep your gigglish games and happy-clappy Trogmanay. I'm just here to warm me whelks. It's sunbathin' for me, in lots and lots of snuggly, goldish sunshi—'

At that moment I looked out of the window. I don't remember much about what happened next, except for seeing something twisting and gigantic crashing up the beach towards the hotel, and the deafening roar as it blew the front door inwards and shattered the windows into a thousand tiny pieces...

WHOOMMFF!

Suddenly everything went white!

Hail and sleet thundered in through the open front door and spiralled up the great staircase, engulfing everyone in seconds.

For a moment the shock of the cold made me catch my breath and I struggled to see as I was hit with blast after blast of rushing snow.

Opening one eye, I found myself lying on the black and white tiles, and I watched in surprise and wonder as fingers of frost crackled across the floor from outside, covering everything in silvery blue swirls and patterns.

'Frankie!' Dad's voice called over the roar from a little way off. I peered through the howling blizzard and saw my parents huddled against the reception desk, half-buried in a snowdrift. 'Frankie, close the door!'

I gritted my teeth, pushed myself up onto my knees and glanced about. Everywhere looked like the churning insides of a ginormous frozen washing machine!

Jagged icicles were erupting in spikes from every ledge and corner, jutting off the staircase and chandeliers. Great-Great-Aunt Zennifer's statue at the centre of the fountain had suddenly become a twisted sculpture of glittering ice, and our smaller guests (mostly the moss gremlins and bogrunts) were spinning through the air, desperately grabbing at anything they could.

I hauled myself along the floor, trying my hardest to keep low and not be flung across the room in the screaming wind, but I could feel myself slipping with every movement.

'AAAAEEEEE!!!'

Gingiva Molar zoomed over my head with an enormous grin on her face, followed by Dentina and Fluora. 'Thith ith amathing!'

At last I reached the base of the front door and scrabbled upwards, trying to find the handle. My fingers grazed across something curved and metallic, and I clutched it as hard as I could.

'Come on, Frankie,' I spluttered to myself as I carefully struggled to my feet. I gripped the edge of the door and pushed as hard as I could against the ferocious gale that still howled in from outside. 'Push!'

As I heaved against the wood, I looked out onto the deserted promenade and couldn't believe what I was seeing.

The daylight had completely disappeared behind the rolling clouds, and the beach was now blanketed in white, like someone had rubbed it out with the end of a giant pencil. Beyond that, the sea was a frozen mass of solid hills and humps and the pier had vanished into the storm.

'Francis!' It was Mum. She rushed up next to me, covering her eyes with her arm, and went to slam the door.

'Wait!' I yelled. I stuck my foot out and stopped it as I spotted something lumbering over the frozen waves towards us. 'Look!'

At first it was almost impossible to make out … just a galloping shape … but, when it reached the shore and started clomping its way up the beach, I realised I was staring at some sort of colossal beast with three riders huddled on its back.

'It's them!' I bawled over the rushing wind.

'Who?' Mum's eyes were enormous with surprise.

'YETIS!!!' I howled and, in my enthusiasm, let go of the door.

WHOOSH!!!

With one last glance at the huge animal making its way towards our front steps, I was hurled backwards into the reception hall, flying face first into a mound of snow with a painful '**HUMPH!**'

7

THEY'RE HERE!

The moment I landed in the freezing-cold snowdrift, I wriggled my head loose and turned to see what was about to trudge through our front door.

For the teensiest of seconds I couldn't see anything out there in the raging storm and wondered if I might have imagined it.

'Where is it?' I said out loud. 'Where is—'

Finally the animal's tremendous silhouette emerged from the blizzard and I felt my eyes nearly pop out of my head as it shambled inside.

The creature was so tall it had to duck to get

under the high archway, and the enormous antlers growing from either side of its head scraped both sides of the door frame. Its plate-sized hooves clanked noisily against the frosty floor tiles and thick clouds of steam huffed out of its bulbous nostrils.

I had spent my whole life rifling through Great-Great-Great-Grandad Abe's books of strange and exotic animals in my bedroom, and I'd recognise this one anywhere. It was a hulking Arctic ulk and it

was standing in our reception!

'HOOOOOOOOOOOOOg!' the ulk bellowed above the din. The sound was so deep and loud, I could feel it in my teeth. **'HOOOOOOOOOOOOOg!'**

Just then I remembered the three riders on the massive creature's back and jumped to my feet to get a better look. They were so heavily bundled in blankets with scarves wrapped round their heads that I couldn't actually see a single hint of yeti.

Dad had clambered out of the snow

onto the stone counter and was frantically waving and gesturing up at them, although I couldn't hear what he was yelling over the howling blizzard.

I watched, with my heart pounding in my chest, as the tallest rider at the back of the saddle pulled out a glass jar (about the size of a briny-bean can) from the folds of its shawl and lifted the lid.

All at once the wind stopped and the storm whipped itself into the little container like an airborne whirlpool. The deafening roar was replaced by complete silence and the thousands of snowflakes that were hurtling about the place suddenly froze in mid-air, then floated gently to the ground.

'Ahh, that's better.' The largest yeti replaced the lid of the storm jar with a tiny **CLINK!**

'What's going on?' Mum whimpered at Dad, breaking the sudden quiet, but he was already bounding off the reception desk and sprinting round to the other side of the Artic ulk.

'Orfis, my old friend!'

'Orfis?' Mum blurted.

The middle rider yanked the scarf off his large

head, exposing a furry face split in half by an enormous grin.

'IT'S ME!' the yeti guffawed. 'Turn down the heating, it's boiling in here!'

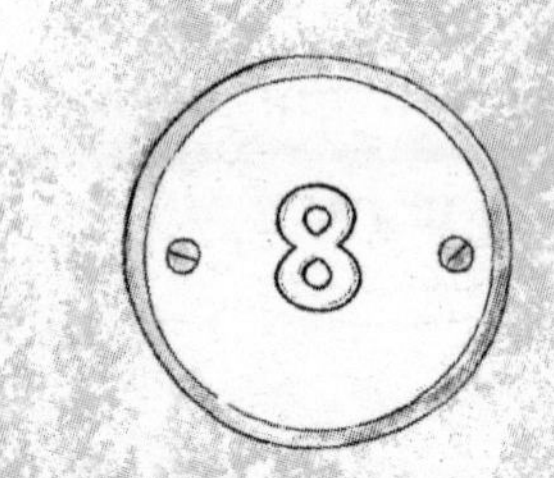

MEET THE KWINZIS

In no time, the three riders had jumped down from the ulk and were busily unwrapping themselves like Trogmanay presents.

It had been so long since I last saw Orfis, I barely recognised him. His brown fur had started to go grey around his chin, and it was much longer and wilder.

'Ooooh! Four thousand five hundred miles on an ulk can give you such sore bumly bits!' The yeti laughed as he raced over to Dad and scooped him up in a tight, hairy hug. 'Bargeous, my furless friend!'

'I DON'T BELIEVE IT!' Mum gawped in surprise, looking like she'd just been trampled by a whole herd of ulks. 'Is it really you?' she spluttered,

wiping snow off her face. 'We had no idea you were coming!'

Dad shot me a cheeky wink.

'We made it!' the tallest yeti boomed in a voice much growlier than Orfis's. She pulled the scarf down from around her face and smiled sweetly.

It was Orfis's wife, Unga.

Female yetis are much larger and stronger than the males. I knew that because I'd read it in the same book where I'd seen the Arctic ulk. Unga's fur was paler in colour than Orfis's, and tinged with turquoise and silver. Most of the hair around her head had been plaited and threaded with little green beads.

'Rani!' Unga said, chuckling to herself and flinging her massive arms open. 'Come over here and give me a squelch.'

'Knot my noggin!' said Orfis as he put Dad down and turned his attention to me. 'This can't be Frankie?'

'Yep!' I said, barely able to stop grinning like a trinx-weasel.

'I can't believe my peepers!' Orfis continued. 'You're a sight for salty eyes, if ever there was one! 'Ere, Unga! Look at how grown-uply our Frankie is!'

Keeping Mum in a great big yeti hug, Unga glanced over at me and practically screamed.

'Oh, my blunkers! The last time I saw you, Frankie, you were tinklier than a twigling!'

'Where's little Zingri?' Dad asked, hopping about like an overexcited puppy.

'She ain't so little any more, Bargeous,' Orfis said. He reached out and pulled the smallest figure towards us. 'This way, loveling.'

The little yeti was still wearing a blanket pulled right up over her head with eyeholes cut in it, but Unga quickly yanked it away.

'Zingri, my lumplet!' Orfis boomed. 'You were a ball of tufty-fluff the last time we were here, so I doubt you'll remember the Banisters. This here is Bargeous, Rani and the littl'un is Frankie.'

Zingri was about two years younger than me, but she was already nearly as tall as my dad. Her hair was white and grey with blue at the ends, like all young yetis. She had a single snaggle-fang poking out from her bottom lip at a wonky angle.

'Cor!' she said, looking around the room with wide eyes and an expression of surprise on her face.

'Well, go on, then,' said Unga, giving her daughter a gentle nudge. 'Say hello, my little nervous nelly.'

'Hello,' Zingri mumbled.

'That's my girl,' Unga said. She planted her enormous paws on her hips and glanced around. 'Well, here we are at the Nothing To See Here Hotel. What a Trogmanay treat!'

I could tell by Zingri's face that she'd never seen anything like our hotel before. She peered up the frozen spiral staircase and...

'The sky is wrong!' Zingri yelped, then darted behind Unga's legs.

'Haha!' Orfis hooted. 'Boogle my brains, I clean forgot. Poor Zingri ain't never seen a ceiling before!'

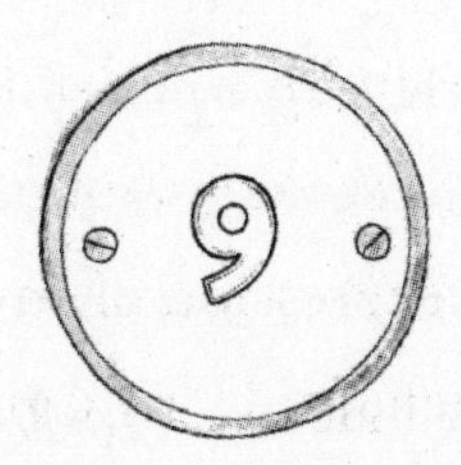

A FROSTY RECEPTION

'I do like what you've done with the place,' Unga said, gazing round the reception hall. 'It's much nicer than the last time we were here.'

'I agree,' said Orfis, snapping an icicle off the nearest picture frame and picking his teeth with it. 'Much frostier. Lovely!'

In all the excitement, I'd completely ignored the aftermath of the wild storm that had just bulldozed through our door and into all our poor guests who'd been suddenly transformed into living ice pops.

It was like we were standing inside a vast igloo. Everything was covered in snow and swirling frost formations. Here and there pairs of waggling legs were sticking up out of the drifts and some of our guests had got themselves trapped behind cages of icy stalagmites.

'Well, that wath a thurprize!' the Molar Sisters cackled from somewhere above us.

Gingiva and Dentina had somehow landed back on the third-floor balcony after being blown about and were busy brushing themselves down, but Fluora was dangling by the elastic of her blue patterned knickers from one of the chandeliers.

'Motht unexthpected!' she chuckled.

The pine dryad's branches were now dusted with snow and glistening. He looked more like a Drooltide tree than one of our paying guests.

'Gosh! Look!' said Dad, pointing at the nearest wall. I glanced over and saw that the vines printed on the enchanted wallpaper were wilting and shrivelling in the cold. The leaf patterns were slowly turning brown and fluttering down the walls. 'Now it really is winter!'

'Lovely juddery weather,' Orfis said with a smile as he inspected the scene.

Grime fairies were playing on the fountain,

sliding down the loops of ice, the moss gremlins were dotted about the floor like startled little snowmen, and the anemononk was busily unpicking his frosty feelers from around the hatstand.

The only guest who didn't seem to have been affected by the storm at all was Madam McCreedie. She was hovering by the open front door, hungrily eyeing a small figure who was coughing and wheezing outside on the top step.

'Who's this?' McCreedie croaked, licking her lips. 'Haven't seen this one before.'

'Oh my goodness,' Dad said, suddenly noticing the creature on the step. 'It's another guest!'

'They must have got caught outside when the storm hit,' said Mum, frowning with worry. I could practically hear the cogs clunking away inside her head. 'Think of the bad reviews...' she was saying to herself.

In case you didn't know, Mum and Dad spend most of their evenings sending fake bad reviews to the local human newspapers. They help to keep nosy tourists from wandering in off the street. The

Nothing To See Here Hotel thrives on TERRIBLE human reviews. Dad even frames the worst ones over reception with pride, but Granny Regurgita would eat us for breakfast if the hotel got a bad reputation among magicals!

Dad helped the little figure hobble inside. It was dragging a large, birdcage-shaped piece of luggage, wrapped tightly in a woven red cloth, and a snow-covered magpie bristled on its shoulder. As it got closer, I could see the creature was a gnomad of some sort, although I wasn't sure exactly what type.

Gnomads are solitary wanderers, which means we rarely have any staying with us. It must have had the shock of its life, being stuck outside when a magic blizzard thundered up the beach. They normally prefer hot climates. Why in the world would a gnomad be in Brighton?

'Do come inside,' Dad said. 'We'll have you warmed up in no time.'

Despite being shrouded in floor-length robes, I could clearly see the gnomad was shivering and its teeth were chattering loudly underneath the oversized clay mask it was wearing.

'I'll just help you with this.' Dad reached out to take the birdcage-shaped luggage from the gnomad, but the magpie on its shoulder suddenly flapped its wings and cawed loudly.

'Handsss off, halfling!' it croaked.

'Sorry,' said Dad, looking alarmed.

'Don't want sssorry!' the bird continued, speaking for its master. 'Want a room. One room for usssssssssss, pleassssssse.'

'Yes! Of course!' Mum said, quickly taking the lead from Dad and hurrying the unfortunate customer over to the reception desk. 'My apologies

for the … umm … appearance of the hotel.'

'The poor little grub,' said Unga. 'It must have been blown about like a bog-bonker out there.'

Mum glanced through the guest logbook, then clapped her hands together.

'You're in luck,' she said, smiling her customer-service smile. 'We have one last room available. It's small, but it has a good view of the beac— umm … snow and you've your own private plunge pond.'

'We'll take it!' the magpie rasped.

'Well, then,' said Mum, with a look that was somewhere between bewilderment and excitement, 'if there are no more surprises, it's high time we got ready for a splendid Trogmanay Trolliday.'

Then she turned in the direction of the kitchen and gasped.

MANKY OLD MALONEY'S CURSE

Mum was staring at a squat lump of snow, right in the middle of the room, next to the lepre-caravan and its gaggle of chilly chickens. The sound of angry muttering was coming from inside it.

'MISS MALONEY!' Mum cried. She darted over to the grumbling mound and, using the hem of her long skirt, started to dust the top part of it away.

'BLURG!' came a high-pitched cry from inside the snow pile, as Maudlin Maloney's grizzled face began to emerge.

I couldn't help but gawp. With her face poking out of the snowy bump, the leprechaun looked like a nightmarish Russian Doll.

'What the **BLUNKERS** is occurrinatin'?!' Maudlin

wheezed. **'SNOW?!'**

'Oh, Miss Maloney!' Mum said. 'We've had a lovely surprise visit from some old yeti friends of ours. Isn't that wonderful?'

'Wonderful?' the leprechaun barked. 'It's disgusterous! Yetis are loathsome, smelly creatures.'

'Oi! I heard that!' Unga snapped. 'I'll have you know I wash and shampoo my hair very regularly … every ten years!'

'I even had a quick de-flea before we came,' Orfis added with a hurt expression.

'RUINED!' Maudlin howled, wriggling this way and that, trying to free herself from the snow. Her dreadlocks were now solid spikes sticking out horizontally from the back of her head. 'Me trolliday is **RUINED!** Where's me sunshine? Where's me warmly weekend? How am I gonna toast me tootsies now?'

'I'm sure we can sort it out,' Mum said nervously. 'A dressing gown or a cup of tea maybe? I'll call Nancy—'

'I ought to hex the lot of you!' Maudlin barked,

freeing a tattooed arm from the snow and pointing one of her gnarled fingers this way and that. **'I'LL WRECK YOUR TROGMANAY, YOU FROSTY FOOLS!'**

'Now I'm sure there's no need for that,' Dad said, raising his hands as if Miss Maloney's bony finger was a loaded pistol.

'NOBODY MOVE!' Maudlin shouted and nobody did.

The unfortunate gnomad's mask only had one eyehole, but I could clearly see a green eye blinking in alarm at the hopping-mad leprechaun. I bet it was wishing it hadn't bothered coming to the

Nothing to See Here Hotel at all!

'We operate a strict no-cursing policy at this hotel,' warned Mum, but Maloney wasn't listening.

'May all your Trogmanay presents be socks!' she screeched.

'No! Stop!' I yelled at her, but it was too late. The foul old fairy had started her curse.

'May your minkle-meat pies taste like dryad droppin's!'

'HOW RUDE!' exclaimed the dryad as his frosty pine needles blushed red.

'May you find yeti hair in every mouthful of termite trifle!'

'Thoundth deliciouth!' the Molar Sisters laughed.

'Please, Miss Maloney! Look, have these to make up for the lack of sunshine!' Dad said, trying to distract the miserable trout with a wad of mud spa vouchers from behind the counter.

'May your barnacle-and-blowfish ice cream always give you brain-freeze!'

'Eh? I love brain-freeze!' Orfis snorted. 'This one's bungled in the bonce!'

'May your nose ooze soup and your soup turn to snot!'

Maudlin was on a roll now! She was so furious that the snow piled up around her was melting into a puddle at her feet.

'May all your teeth fall out, except one! And may that tooth have a cavity!'

'That doethn't thound tho bad!' lisped the Molar Sisters.

'I think that's quite enough,' Dad ordered, trying to look tough and not like he was scared out of his wits.

'May your bottom forever be prickled by thorns and your arms shrink so you can't scratch it!!'

'WHAT?!' Mum yelped.

'May you always have unwelcome guests at your festive table!'

Maloney took an enormous deep breath. I could tell she was winding herself up for her worst curses yet.

'May your roasted trog hog always be dry!' Maudlin was practically spitting the words at us.

'May your tongues turn to wood so you can't taste the delunktious feast, and may you always run out of extra-thick and spicy mango chutney!'

'THAT'S IT!' Unga roared so ferociously that even Miss Maloney looked frightened for a second. The yeti marched over to the ancient bad-luck fairy and loomed over her.

'You can hex our Trogmanay presents,' Unga continued. 'You can tricksy our trifles and meddle with the minkle-meat, **BUT DON'T YOU EVER MESS WITH THE ROAST TROG HOG AND MANGO CHUTNEY!'**

With that, Unga reached back into the folds of her shawl and pulled out the glass storm jar. 'Now bog off, you scabberous old skrunt!'

In an instant, Unga yanked off the lid.

'AAAAAAGH!'

There was an almighty WHOOOSH! and a blur of leprechaun shot backwards across the reception hall like a leathery Catherine wheel. Maudlin Maloney zoomed straight through the open front door of her caravan, vanishing inside.

'And stay in there!' Unga shouted.

For a second everyone held their breath … half-expecting Maloney to explode back out at us. So we all heaved a sigh of relief when we eventually heard her angrily muttering to herself from inside and the sound of a kettle being put on the burner. It looked like she'd learned her lesson. For now…

'That's that, then,' Unga said, dusting off her palms like she'd finished doing chores. 'Who's up for a snowball fight and hot mug of trog nog?'

YOU'VE MADE IT THIS FAR

Chapter Eleven!! Would you ever have believed that you'd have stuck with me and my weird family for this long?

So far, so strange, right?

Well, I'll let you in on a secret…

After being woken with the threat of a 'right pickle', nearly getting crushed by a chicken - powered caravan, seeing my first leprechaun, being half-frozen by a magical blizzard, witnessing the arrival of yetis on an Arctic ulk, discovering a frostbitten gnomad on the doorstep and getting well and truly cursed, I was pretty certain things couldn't get any stranger … at least for the rest of the day.

BUT I WAS SO WRONG!

Don't go anywhere, my friend.

If you think what you've read so far is loop-de-loop crazy, you won't believe what happened later that evening.

Brace yourself…

LET THE FESTIVITIES BEGIN!

'This way!' I huffed over my shoulder as I ran down the corridor, with Zingri bounding along behind me.

After all the earlier madness, Mum had sprung into action and started barking orders, making preparations for tonight's Trogmanay feast. Cursed or not, there was no way she was going to let our trolliday weekend be a disappointment.

Nancy made quick work of knitting scarves and woolly hats for everyone, while Ooof was put in charge of leading the Arctic ulk out to the gardens to graze in the snow. Dad took Orfis and Unga for a drop of bluebottle brandy in the library and I was given the afternoon off to show Zingri round the hotel.

The only person who refused to join in the fun was Great-Great-Great-Granny Regurgita. I called her room on the yell-a-phone to say the Kwinzis were staying with us, but she just told me to, 'BOG OFF, WHELP!'

So that was my one job done for the day. BRILLIANT!

'Wait till you see this,' I said as we turned the corner near the dining room.

We'd already been up to the observatorium to look out over the frozen ocean and see how far the storm had stretched, then we slid all the way down the banister of the great staircase and now we were heading outside.

'You'll love it,' I said, pushing open the kitchen door and ducking as a ladle of hot soup flew over my head and clattered against the hallway wall. 'Just through here.'

Nancy had finished her knitting and was whizzing about at the stove, getting ready for tonight's feast. As always, her arms were a blur of whisking, stirring, flipping and chopping. One of her back legs was stretched across the room, carefully turning the trog hog on a spit over the roaring fireplace, and another was churning squirrel milk into butter in a bucket down by her side.

'Nancy,' I said, 'this is Zingri.'

'Oh, how lovely to meet you properly, my wee lamb,' Nancy cooed, barely looking up from her cooking. 'I hope you're hungry!'

'Nice to meet you too,' Zingri replied. 'Yes! It looks … it looks belly-bungling!' Her eyes were the size of saucers. I don't think yetis eat much more than stewed mountain goat up in the Himalayas, so the sight of all this food being prepared must have tinkled her tummy.

'Between you and me, I'm having terrible trouble, Frankie,' Nancy said, furiously stirring a huge pot of bubbling green liquid. 'I don't know why, but my sea-scum soup seems to have turned into snot!'

Zingri glanced at me and let loose a giggle.

'Oh no,' I said and grabbed my new yeti

friend by the arm.

Poor Nancy had missed Maudlin Maloney's rant and had no idea that some of her best dishes had been hexed. I didn't have the heart to tell her that the minkle-meat pies were probably going to taste like dryad droppings as well.

'What a mystery,' I said, secretly thanking my lucky stars that Unga had stopped the leprechaun when she did. 'Errrm … don't let the trog hog dry out, will you?'

I yanked Zingri towards the conservatory door and we bolted off in the direction of the patio by the pool.

We sprinted along the rows of Mr Croakum's plant pots until Zingri stopped in her tracks when we reached the far door and gasped.

Everything outside in the garden looked INCREDIBLE!

The lanterns had been lit in the trees and the hundreds of birdhouse-sized boxes that lined their branches had been brightly decorated by their piskie inhabitants.

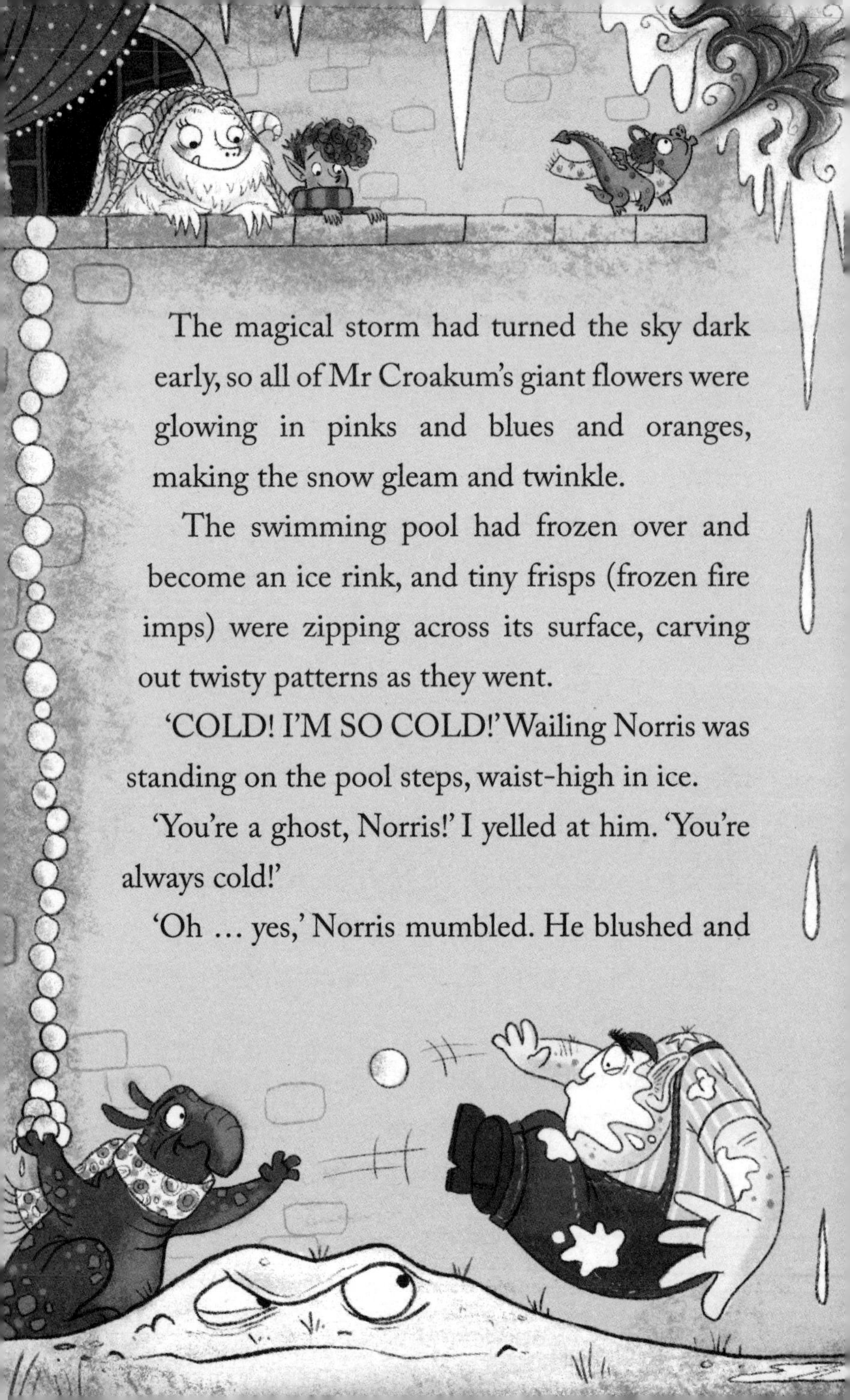

The magical storm had turned the sky dark early, so all of Mr Croakum's giant flowers were glowing in pinks and blues and oranges, making the snow gleam and twinkle.

The swimming pool had frozen over and become an ice rink, and tiny frisps (frozen fire imps) were zipping across its surface, carving out twisty patterns as they went.

'COLD! I'M SO COLD!' Wailing Norris was standing on the pool steps, waist-high in ice.

'You're a ghost, Norris!' I yelled at him. 'You're always cold!'

'Oh … yes,' Norris mumbled. He blushed and

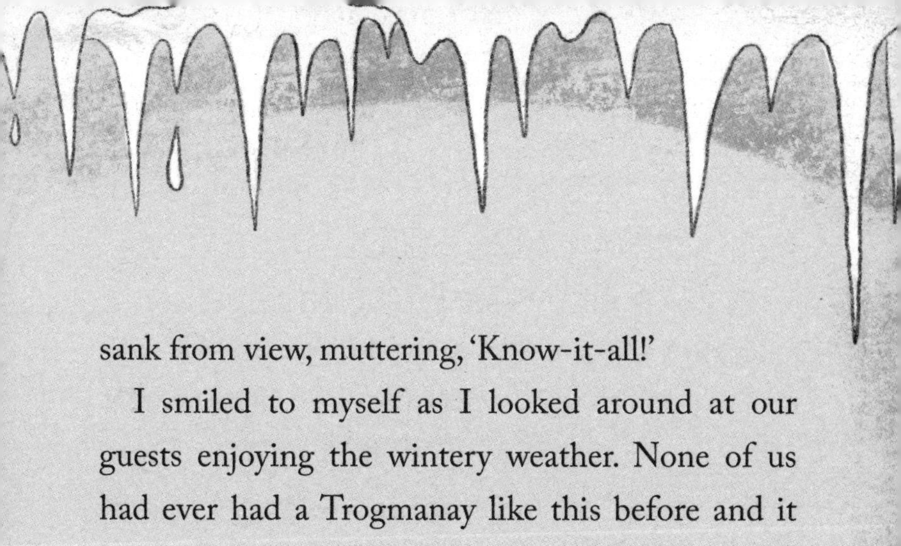

sank from view, muttering, 'Know-it-all!'

I smiled to myself as I looked around at our guests enjoying the wintery weather. None of us had ever had a Trogmanay like this before and it was a relief to see that everyone seemed to be having fun even though it wasn't sunny and warm.

Berol Dunch was bundled up in a blanket at the top of the waterslide. She had a hot-water bottle in her lap and was licking fish skeletons like they were ice pops.

'This reminds me of the time I turned left at

Greenland by mistake,' she said, slurping down chunks of frozen sardine heads. 'I didn't notice until I was practically run over by an iceberg!'

Gladys Potts was chasing snowflakes this way and that in full poodle form, and the Molar Sisters were lying on the floor, making snow fairies.

'It's terrific!' Zingri laughed. 'I've never seen so many unfurry people!'

'Well, there's plenty more to see,' I said and led her to the patio wall to look down at the garden below.

Moss gremlins were swinging on the Arctic ulk's antlers as it munched away at the compost heap, the impolump from this morning was having a snowball fight with Ooof and Hoggit was galloping about, melting icicles that hung below the enchanted benches as they floated past.

'Haha! We have snow all the time, but our village isn't nearly as much fun as this!' Zingri said.

''Ere, am I dreaming?' The Lawn suddenly grunted, making Zingri's eyes widen with surprise. 'Winter? It was sunny when I nodded off!' the old grassghast grumbled. Someone had built a snowgoblin on the Lawn's head and he was frantically nodding from side to side, trying to topple it. 'How long have I been asleep?'

A TURN FOR THE WORSE

'Frankie?' Mum called as she stepped out from the conservatory with a tray filled with steaming mugs of trog nog. 'Ah, there you are!'

She was wearing about ten cardigans, one on top of the other, and looked like she was turning into a stressed, human Trogmanay bauble. There were bits of tinsel sticking out of her hair and a smudge of glitter on her cheek from where she'd obviously been frantically decorating the dining room.

'Frankie, take Zingri and get yourselves dressed for the feast,' she said as she started handing out the drinks to our greedy guests who came flocking from all corners of the garden. 'Nancy's nearly finished cooking and I want you both looking your best for the party!'

'Oh! But, Mum...' I grumbled. I wasn't about to leave all the fun just to go and put a scratchy shirt on!

'No "BUTS", mister!' Mum shot back. 'I want everything to be perfect tonight and that means you looking presentable.'

'I do look presentable!' I said.

Mum raised an eyebrow.

'I look fine! Oh...' I glanced down and realised I was still wearing my pyjamas from this morning. All the rush of Nancy's early wake-up call and our unexpected guests had made me completely forget.

'Well?' Mum said, pulling her 'I'm always right' face. 'Off you go.'

Finally having to admit defeat, I went back inside with Zingri and we headed for my room.

I'd never got changed so quickly in my life!

As fast as I could, I put on my purple jacket, short trousers and Great-Great-Great-Grandad Abe's favourite socks and was ready to go.

'Done!' Zingri said, admiring herself in the mirror. Yetis don't wear clothes, so she'd taken even less time than I had and just thrown on a necklace made from little bones and tied her hair up in a knot on the top of her head. 'Let's go back downstairs!'

We both jumped into the armchair in the corner of the room and sat down. I clicked the combination into the dial on its arm and the chair juddered downwards.

We had nearly made it to the floor, when…

'Look!' Zingri whispered, pointing at the open library doors. There was the gnomad with the magpie on its shoulder. It hadn't spotted us and it looked like the creature and the bird were peeking round the door frame at something in reception.

'Hello!' I called and the gnomad spun round, blinking a green eye at us through the single hole in its mask. 'Are you okay?'

The magpie bristled its feathers and wriggled its talons.

'Sssneaksss!' it hissed. 'Ssscaresss usss!'

'Sorry!' I said, wondering why the gnomad and the bird were still here and hadn't just upped and left after the terrible welcome they'd received earlier that day.

'Sssneaksss make usss jump!' the magpie said. 'Ssstealing, ssslinking tiptoersss!'

'Are you looking for something?' I asked, trying to be polite.

'Frankie…' Zingri said. She was obviously feeling as awkward as I was. 'I think we should … ummm …'

I was just about to make up an excuse so we could get away from the creature and its bad-tempered bird, when the magpie said something I wasn't expecting.

'Ssscreamsss,' it croaked.

'Pardon?' I said.

'Ssscreamsss and sssadnesss. The end of the Nothing To SSSee Here Hotel.'

I gawped at the strange pair for a moment, looking from the gnomad's green eye to the black

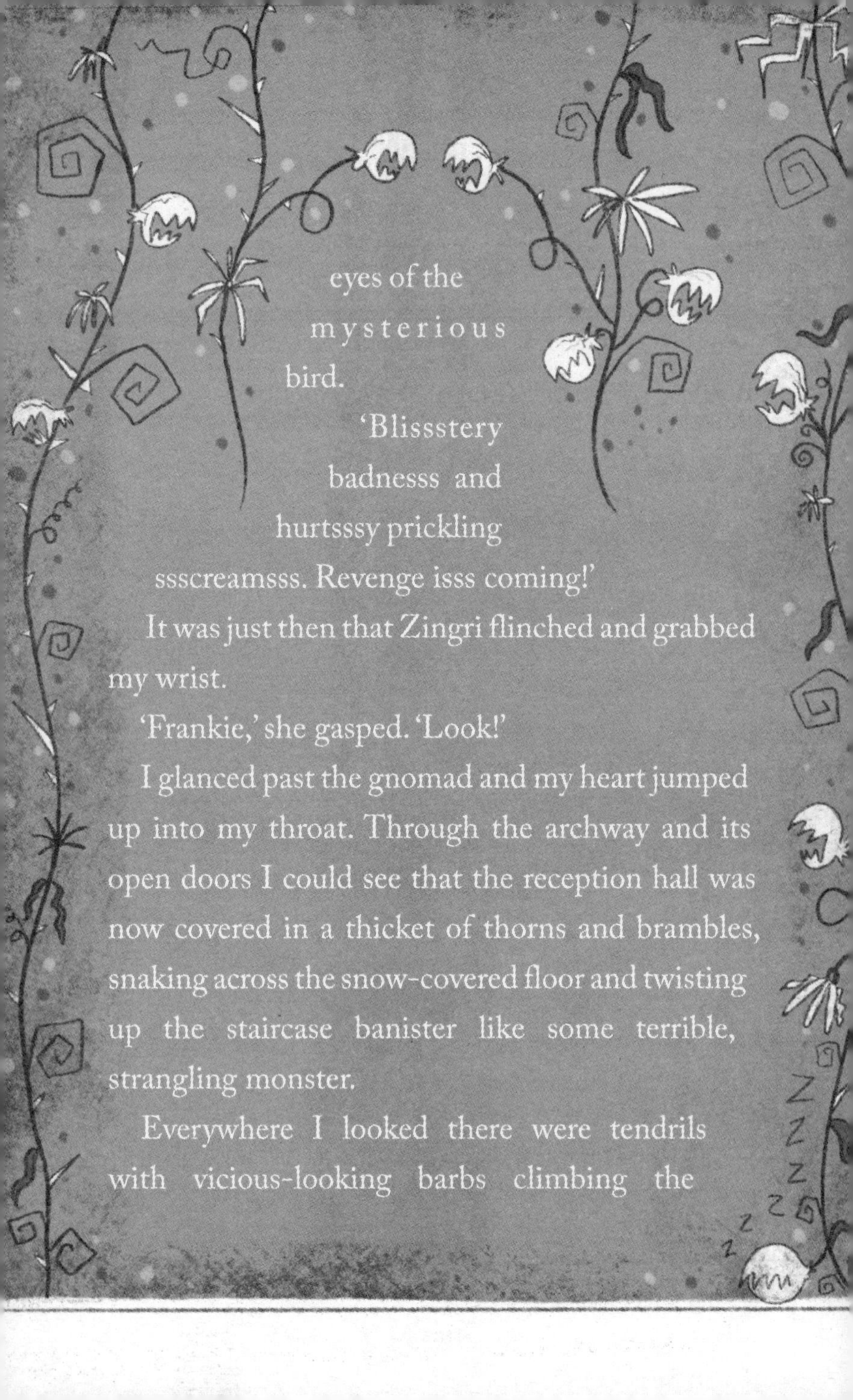

eyes of the mysterious bird.

'Blissstery badnesss and hurtsssy prickling ssscreamsss. Revenge isss coming!'

It was just then that Zingri flinched and grabbed my wrist.

'Frankie,' she gasped. 'Look!'

I glanced past the gnomad and my heart jumped up into my throat. Through the archway and its open doors I could see that the reception hall was now covered in a thicket of thorns and brambles, snaking across the snow-covered floor and twisting up the staircase banister like some terrible, strangling monster.

Everywhere I looked there were tendrils with vicious-looking barbs climbing the

archways
and twitching
from the chandeliers.

The vine patterns on the enchanted wallpaper that we'd watched wither and die in the bitter cold had suddenly sprung back to life and were covered in huge spikes with jagged, ugly leaves. Where there had been pretty flowers, there were gnashing fly-traps that squirmed across the walls.

Walking into the centre of the room, I saw the web of briars was sprouting from a vase on the stone counter. Hadn't there been dead flowers in that earlier? I seemed to remember Mum fussing over it before Maudlin Maloney had come crashing in through the sky door.

MAUDLIN MALONEY! This had to have something to do with her curses! I turned round and there she was, the grizzly old grunion, sitting on the front stoop of her caravan, stirring a small cauldron over a fire she'd made in the snow.

'Well, this is odd, isn't it?' she said, leering a wonky smile. 'What a strange to-do!'

'You did this!' I yelled.

'Nonkumbumps!' she barked back. 'I've been mindin' me own peas and carrots, cookin' up a spot of supper.' She licked the spoon and smacked her cracked lips together. 'Glow-worm gumbo – want to try some?'

'Don't change the subject! I know this was you!'

'Nope, not me!' Maudlin snickered. 'Not old Maloney!'

'Of course it was,' I said. 'Dead flowers don't just sprout thorns and grow all over the place on their own.'

'The gnomad saw everything,' Zingri said as she marched up next to me.

'Ha! I'm sure he did,' Maloney cackled.

I looked back to where the creature and its bird had been standing, but the gnomad was gone.

'It warned Frankie,' Zingri continued. 'It said there would be hurtsy prickling screams.'

'Maybe there will be,' Maudlin said, staring at me with a wicked twinkle in her eye. 'From the looks of all this, I'd say you're all in a whoppsy big tangle of trouble.'

'You don't scare me, you mean old foozle-fart!' I cried.

'Careful, boy,' Miss Maloney said through gritted teeth. 'You wouldn't want to upset a leprechaun, now would you?'

'I don't care!' I bellowed. I was so furious, I could have swung the horrible fairy by her dreadlocks and thrown her straight out of the front door. 'I don't care if you curse the soup, or make our trog hog dry, or cover the whole hotel in thorns! **YOU WON'T RUIN OUR TROLLIDAY!**'

With that, I grabbed Zingri and we ran off towards the dining room.

'Have a lovely dinner!' Maudlin called after us with a sickening chuckle. 'I hope everyone feasts until their bellies burst!'

THE DINING ROOM

'We have to tell Mum and Dad,' I wheezed as we ran along. 'Maloney can't get away with it!'

'Ignore her,' Zingri huffed as we left the leprechaun's laughter behind us. 'She's only trying to bonejangle you! Don't let her ruin your dinner.'

Now, I should probably explain a few things before we carry on…

I know you'll be imagining the Trogmanay feast in our dining room, even though I haven't started describing it. Admit it, you are, aren't you?

I knew it!

You've already heard how big the Nothing To See Here Hotel is, and how greedy our guests are, so you'll be picturing a ginormous room filled to the rafters with fancy tables and chairs and buffet carts and chocolate fountains, ready for hordes of starvatious guests, right?

WRONG!

If you and your family checked in for Trogmanay and headed straight off to join the feast, you'd be shocked when you walked through the dining room door and found yourself looking at just one single table and only one chair.

The table would be piled high with Nancy's tummy-tinkling food, and even though she's cooked **LOADS** it wouldn't look nearly enough for over a hundred gorgesome guests, **AND** there's only one knife and fork with jade-green handles.

'What's going on?' you'd say to yourself, scratching your head and wondering if there'd been some terrible mix-up. But there's no mistake, I promise you.

Unlike you polite and well-behaved humans, on special occasions we magicals don't eat **AT** the table … we eat **ON** the table.

Haha! You weren't expecting that, were you?

At extra-special dinners all the guests line up and, one by one, they sit in the chair. Then, picking up the knife and fork, they bang the jade handles on the table and, with a clear voice, shout the one magical word that shrinks them down to the size of a squinkel nugget.

'HONKSWALLOP!'

FLASH! ZIPP! POOOOF! PING! and it's done!

In no time at all, every single guest is teeny-tiny and clambering over the feast, burrowing their way into a towering crustacean cake drizzled with toads' tears or chomping into a minkle-meatball that's three times the size of their head.

BRILLIANT!

A TROGMANAY FEAST TO REMEMBER

Zingri and I reached the dining room door just as Nancy was ushering in the last of the guests.

'Oh! There you are, duckies,' she said, spotting us sprinting towards her.

'Nancy!' I panted, trying to catch my breath. 'Where are Mum and Dad? I need to talk to them.'

'They're already on the table,' Nancy said, smiling sweetly and batting her eight eyelids with glee. 'Hurry now or you'll both miss the trog-roast toast.'

'Quick!' I said to Zingri.

Inside the dining room, the food looked honkhumptious. The table was piled high with bowls of fried snatchling steaks, squashed pigeon porridge, hashed brownies, tangle-root rostis, hot and crumbly dung-beetle muffins with trunkum-fruit jelly, curried mud-whifflers, porcupatties smothered in sticky giblet jam! You name it, Nancy had cooked it, and, dotted around the huge plates and platters of delunktious delicacies, were hundreds of miniature magicals.

I saw Orfis and Unga straight away because they were twice as tall as all the others – about the size of my thumb – and I knew that Mum and Dad were probably somewhere close by.

Zingri went first and, once she'd swizzled down to nothing but a speck of fluff on the tablecloth, I sat in the chair and picked up the knife and fork.

Shrinking for a festive feast was normally one of my favourite things to do, and I felt a stab of anger that Maudlin Maloney was spoiling it. The quicker I told Mum and Dad, the quicker they could have Ooof throw the crooked crone out and we could enjoy our feast properly.

'HONKSWALLOP!' I shouted as loudly as I could, banging the jade handles on the table.

A tingling sensation shot up and down my spine,

and my fingers crackled as the magic spell took hold. The whole room suddenly stretched and twisted like jelly.

Shrinking is sort of like falling, only instead of plummeting downwards, the ground rushes up to meet you.

'Uhhhfff!' I came to an abrupt stop and found myself standing at the edge of the table with mountains of food in front of me. What had been dishes of sauce and slabs of cheese only seconds ago were now the size of lakes and cathedrals.

I spotted Orfis and Unga a little way off, and could see Zingri was already lumbering over to them, so I followed as fast as I could. As I got nearer, Dad

came into view, standing on the rim of a bowl filled with pocket-lint fritters. He was getting ready to make his trolliday speech.

'Excuse me!' I ran through the guests, darting this way and that, trying to get to my parents as quickly as I could. 'Excuse me!'

'Ladies and gentlemen!' Dad called over the chitter-chatter.

'And tooth fairieth!' the Molar Sisters piped up.

'And impolumps!'

'And werepoodles!'

'EVERYONE!' Dad yelled, cutting off the rest of the crowd before anyone else could join in. 'It is with happiness in my haunches and armfuls of Trogmanay cheer that I'd like to welcome you all to our summery … ermm … wintery trog-hog feast.'

A cheer went up from all our guests.

'Firstly, I'd like to make a special trog-roast toast to Nancy and all her delinktible cooking!'

Everyone raised their glasses and turned to face the gargantuan spider. She was still full-size and loomed over us like a titan with a purple perm.

'OH, YOU'RE TOO SWEET!' Nancy boomed, making the entire table shake.

We all clamped our hands over our ears and cowered at the deafening noise.

''Ere, keep it down!' the pine dryad pleaded with a painful expression.

'Oh, sorry,' Nancy whispered as quietly as an exploding volcano. 'Thank you, my lovelies. Now, before we get started, does anyone need anything? Any last orders?'

'Where's the mango chutney?' Gladys Potts called up to her. 'I can't see it anywhere!'

Nancy's eight eyes scanned the table, then she gasped and clutched her four hands to her chest.

'Goodness me,' she exclaimed. 'What a wally-wonk I am! Back in a jiffy!'

Nancy turned and hurried out of the room with footsteps as loud as thunder, and...

I couldn't be certain, but I thought I caught a glimpse of the gnomad and its magpie peeking round the edge of the door as it creaked shut.

That thing is SO weird, I thought to myself.

Gnomads don't eat anything at all, so it must have been feeling pretty left out right about then. If it wasn't so grumpy, I might even have felt sorry for the little creature.

'Moving on!' Dad shouted, breaking my train of thought. 'Without any further ado, I wish you all the happiest of magical new years and I hope you all enjoy THE FEAST!'

With that, everybody darted off in different directions like bugs that had just been discovered under a log.

In seconds, guests and staff alike were sliding down the dandruff-dusted doughsticks, bouncing on the beetle-brain buns and taking a luxurious dip in the chinchilla-cheese fondue.

'Thith ith thmashing!' the Molar Sisters hooted between enormous mouthfuls as they devoured the three corners of a dragon-breath chilli tortilla chip. After a few seconds, they each threw their heads back and belched flames into the air. 'Thpicy!'

Watching with a mixture of excitement and nervousness as people bustled this way and that, I headed over to where Mum and Dad were standing.

Part of me desperately wanted to dive head first into a nearby tray of mouth-marvelling hashed brownies that were as big as sofa cushions, but I had to let my parents know what Maudlin Maloney had done to reception and about the gnomad's warning.

I ran round the edge of the gigantic termite trifle and was nearly swept off my feet as Gladys Potts galloped past, dragging a snatchling steak the size of a duvet behind her.

'Darling!' Mum's voice suddenly called over the din. 'There you are!'

My parents and the Kwinzis were standing by the mountainous slices of roast trog hog and balls of sage-and-bunion stuffing.

'Here's our little Frankie!' Unga chuckled. She was hugging Zingri, who'd got to them ahead of me.

'Where've you been?' Dad asked as I ran over.

'We thought you weren't coming, my little lump,' Orfis said, planting a big kiss on the top of my head.

'Mum! Dad!' I said. 'Something awful—'

'We know,' Mum interrupted me. 'Zingri's just been telling us.'

'Thorns all over reception?' Dad asked. 'What a mess!'

'Yes,' I said. 'Maudlin Maloney is plotting her revenge. I think she's going to do something even more terrible.'

'Oh, don't exaggerate, Francis!' Mum said, rolling her eyes. 'Honestly! She's just a great big gasbag.'

'But her curses are coming true!' I huffed. 'She said, "May our bottoms be prickled by thorns," and now reception is covered in briars. Nancy's soup turned to snot!'

'Well, not all of them are coming true,' Mum said. She was normally the biggest stress-head of all and she didn't seem to be worried in the slightest. Why wasn't she panicking?

Before I could say another word, Dad grabbed a chunk of trog-hog meat and handed it to me.

'Try it,' he said, giving me an encouraging wink. 'Go on.'

I cautiously took the lump of meat in both hands

and stared at it. It was the size of one of my Real-life Adventures of Calamitus Plank comics.

I bit off a piece and chewed it. It was … DELUNKTIOUS!

The trog hog was juicy and tender and fatty. It was probably the best Trogmanay roast Nancy had ever made. For a second I thought I might cry with happiness as I gulped and swallowed the fantastically moist mouthful of food.

'See!' Mum said. 'There's nothing to worry about.'

'It's amazing,' I said. 'But I don't understand what this has to do with Maloney?'

'That lanksome leprechaun cursed the trog hog,' Unga said. 'But it's squinkly and moresome and not a bit dry.'

'Precisely!' Dad joined in. 'Maloney's lost her touch. She's getting old and so are her hexes.'

'But the gnomad warned me and Zingri that something dreadful was going to happen!' I exclaimed.

'It's true,' Zingri said.

Mum and Dad exchanged a quick concerned

glance.

'Well, I'm sure it was talking about the vines, so it's done now,' Dad said. 'I'll get Ooof to get rid of them after dinner.'

'Let's hope it's all over,' Mum said, suddenly looking a little nervous. 'Everybody's here at least, so we know Maloney's curse about unwelcome guests at the festive table hasn't worked…'

UNWELCOME DINNER GUESTS

Fa-Dunk! Fa-Dunk! Fa-Dunk!

The noise was distant and low at first, but it rumbled menacingly off the dining-room walls and made everybody stop what they were doing to listen.

Fa-Dunk! Fa-Dunk! Fa-Dunk!

'What's that?' asked Zingri.

'It's probably just Nancy coming back with the mango chutney,' Mum replied.

FA-DUNK! FA-DUNK! FA-DUNK!

Unless my ears were playing tricks on me, the sound was getting louder. It seemed to be coming from underneath our feet, like something was shuffling about on the floor.

FA-DUNK! FA-DUNK! FA-DUNK!

There was an ear-shattering squeal as something nudged the chair backwards away from the table and everyone cried out in alarm.

Fa-Dunk! Fa-Dunk! Fa-Dunk!

The sound was different now ... softer! Whatever was down there had just hopped up onto the chair.

'Can you see what it is?' Mum said. 'If it's Hoggit snaffling for scraps, there's going to be trouble.'

I walked to the edge of the table and nervously peered over, being careful to keep my balance. Far below on the wooden seat were three leathery brownish lumps. If I had been normal-sized, they'd each be about the size of an apple, but right now they were as big as hot-air balloons.

'What can you see, Frankie?' Dad called over to me. 'Anything?'

I was about to yell back to Dad and say I thought they were extra-large minkle-meatballs when the middle one opened its yellow eyes and glowered up at me.

After that, everything was a bit of a blur if I'm

honest. I barely had time to run back from the edge before…

FA-DUNK! FA-DUNK! FA-DUNK!

I dived out of the way as the monstrous things bounced up onto the table with deafening booms! Scurrying back towards my family, I spun round to get a good look…

I recognised all three of them instantly. They were the disgusterous bad-luck charms we'd seen strung to Maudlin Maloney's belt, and now the shrunken heads – which were not so shrunken any more – were very much alive and, by the looks of things, ready to have a feast of their own.

Everybody froze in terror. In our tiny state, the gruesome little lumps were COLOSSAL and towered above us all.

'BLAAAAAGH!' one of the heads groaned, lolling a black tongue out of its mouth and dragging it across jagged teeth.

'BROOOOAAAAAAAAAHHH!' the heads roared and all at once chaos broke out across the tabletop.

'Run fer it!' Orfis howled as the head with a ring through its nose bounced towards us with its mouth open wide. 'THEY'RE TRYING TO EAT US!'

CRASH!

The head landed on the edge of the trog-hog platter, sending boulder-sized balls of sage-and-bunion stuffing bouncing high into the air.

'Go, go, go!' Dad yelled, grabbing me by the arm and dragging me away as the shrunken head flopped out its crusty tongue again. 'Get to higher ground!'

Ahead of me, I could see Mum and the Kwinzis sprinting across the tablecloth as balls of stuffing came thundering down like dreadful savoury bombs.

'OOOF NO LIKE!' Ooof bawled as we passed him. He swung a breadstick like a club and knocked one of the gruesome heads over on its side. It was the super-leathery one that Maudlin Maloney had introduced as her Aunt Influenza. For a second I thought our handyogre might just have defeated it, until the horrible thing wobbled upright and screamed in Ooof's face, sending a green cloud of rancid breath billowing out in front of it.

Dad and I raced round an immense jug of grappleweed gravy and came face to face with the third horrible head. It had a patch over one eye and the faded remains of a blue anchor tattooed on its chin which meant that this dreadful thing had once been a Squall Goblin, just like Captain Calamitus Plank.

'**GAAAAAAAAH!**' it bellowed so loudly that the tabletop rumbled under our feet. '**BLAAAAARRG!**'

'Over here, Frankie!' Dad yelled as he pulled me up onto a great hill of crab-curd koftas. 'Get to the top!'

I scrambled as fast as I could, but the enormous fried blocks of food were greasy and it was difficult to grip the edges as I climbed.

'This way, grub!' Unga called to me. She was a few levels higher on the stack of crispy snacks and I could see she'd already helped Mum, Orfis and Zingri up onto the pile. 'Wiffly now! As quinkly as you can!'

She reached down and grabbed me by my jacket

collar, then lifted me straight up to the top of the crunchy peak.

'THIS IS DISASTEROUS!' Orfis howled as a plate of iced bumble-wheat buns was upended and they crashed into the side of our food mountain like meteors. 'We're gonelies!'

From the top of the crab-curd koftas I could see the terrible scene unfolding all around me. It was like everything was moving in slow motion…

I watched as the ugly blob with the ring through its nose cornered Reginald Blink and his family by the dish of rat-tail terrine. With one foul **SLUUURRPP**, it sucked them all straight off their feet and gobbled all four of them down at once.

Aunt Influenza's head was now splashing about in the cauldron of cursed snotty soup like some nightmarish tea bag. It was guzzling down mouthfuls of the green liquid, then spitting jets of it back out as guests ran past in a panic, sending them flying across the table.

'Aaaeeeeeeee!' I turned just in time to see the

pirate head blow an almighty gust of wind at Berol Dunch who had somehow shimmied up a drinking straw to escape the chaos.

The geriatric mermaid spiralled into the air, flapping her fishtail this way and that. Then, as she started to fall back down, the tattooed head bounced up towards her and swallowed her whole with a reverberating **GULP!**

JUST IN THE NICK OF TIME

Hope seemed to be running out faster than you could scream, 'PLEASE DON'T EAT ME!'

In only a few minutes, the three gruesome heads had gleefully gobbled down half our guests and were showing no signs of stopping.

'AAAAGH!' Gladys Potts was seized off the top of the dung-beetle muffins.

'NOOOOO!' Madam McCreedie was sniffed up Aunt Influenza's nose as she flew frantically past.

'GUUUUHH!' Ooof was licked right off the tablecloth and vanished down the pirate head's slimy throat before he'd even realised it was behind him.

This is it! I thought as I stared with wide eyes. *Maudlin Maloney is winning. The gnomad and its magpie were right and this is the end of the Nothing To See Here Hotel.*

Aunt Influenza's head had been busily slurping back the family of bogrunts, who'd swum out into the centre of the pork-and-parsley punchbowl for safety, when the gory lump swivelled its eyes upwards and spotted us all huddled at the top of the still wobbling crab-curd koftas.

A crooked leer spread across its withered face and it started to bounce towards us.

FA-DUNK! FA-DUNK!

BOOOOOOOOM!

A second much louder noise suddenly echoed round the cavernous dining room. Even the three heads stopped hopping about and seemed to listen for a moment, despite their ears being stuffed full of old rags and sawdust.

BOOOOOOOOM! BOOOOOOOOM! BOOOOOOOOM!

My heart sank in despair. What was Maloney

sending to get us now?

BOOOOOOOOM! BOOOOOOOOM! BOOOOOOOOM!

Suddenly the dining-room door opened and the giant figure of Nancy stepped inside, brandishing a skyscraper-sized bottle of mango chutney.

'FOUND IT, MY WEE BEAUTIES!' she thundered joyfully. **'SORRY I TOOK SO LONG. I'D LEFT IT ON THE—'**

Nancy's mouth drooped open as she stared down at the nearly empty table and three shrivelled heads staring back at her.

If it was possible for a shrunken head to look sheepish, this was the moment. I swear they'd have started twiddling their thumbs if they'd had any.

Nancy turned her attention to the head with a ring through its nose and gasped when she saw the pine dryad's feet … or roots … sticking out of its crusty mouth.

'Mmmmmhhh … mmmmmhhh!' he called from somewhere inside the ghastly thing. 'HUWP MEH!'

That was it…

'OH, BLUNKERS!' Nancy roared, darting forward and snatching up the jade knife and fork from the corner of the table.

There was a tremendous flash of light and a loud WHOOOSHing sound as Nancy snapped the magical cutlery in half.

'UUUUUUUUGH!'

Every single guest who had been celebrating was suddenly un-shrunk.

The three monstrous heads exploded into nothing but clouds of dust and papery flakes of dead skin, as the unfortunate magical creatures packing their gobblesome gullets returned to full size.

Arms and legs flailed in all directions as the table collapsed under our weight. The room instantly filled up and all the guests spilled out into the hallway like a living, breathing avalanche.

'LOCK HER UP!'

'Frankie, my boy,' Nancy's voice sobbed somewhere in the distance. 'Where are you?'

I found myself lying in a pile of wriggling guests with someone's knee wedged against my ear and one of the anemononk's tentacles slapped across my forehead.

'I'm here!' I grunted, feeling like someone had reached inside my skull and scrambled my brains with an egg whisk.

'Oh, petal,' Nancy said, carefully scooping me out of the squirming jumble of guests and putting me down on my feet next to her. 'What on earth?'

I looked up into Nancy's eight eyes and tried to focus. The room felt like it was spinning.

'Ummm,' I mumbled as my thoughts swam around inside my head. 'There was screaming…'

'Right?'

'And thorns … revenge…'

'You're not making much sense, dearie,' Nancy said, placing two of her hands on my shoulders. 'Think, Frankie. What happened?'

'Heads!' I blurted as the image of gristly Aunt Influenza sprang back to my mind. 'Shrunken heads! Giant ones! MAUDLIN MALONEY! We have to stop her!'

As fast as we could, Nancy and I untangled everyone from the pile.

'This way … no, that's your arm … just twist your foot to the left a bit, that's right … pull it out of Ooof's nostril!'

We found Orfis and Unga lying dazed on the splintered remains of the dining table, while Mum, Dad and Zingri had been swept out into the corridor.

Apart from the odd black eye and slobber-drenched hairdo, all of our guests were somehow pretty much unharmed, but BOY, WERE THEY FUMING! I'd never seen magicals look so hopping mad.

'Tell them, Frankie!' Mum said, rubbing a sore spot on her arm. 'Tell them what you know!'

I quickly explained to everyone the gnomad's warnings about the hotel being in danger and how it seemed that Miss Maloney's curses were coming true. She was obviously SO ANGRY that her summer-holiday plans had been ruined and had sent her unlucky charms to ruin our Trogmanay feast and cause chaos.

'Who does she think she is? The cantunkerous turnip!' Reginald Blink huffed.

'That tricksy old trog-stomper!' the impolump grunted, twitching his nose with rage.

'Something's got to be done,' barked Gladys Potts.

'I'll happily eat her,' Madam McCreedie said. 'Call it a favour—'

'NO!' Mum interrupted. 'I won't have any guests being eaten … not again!'

'But we can't let her get away with more of these horrible happenings!' Nancy said as determination spread across her spider-face. 'I know just what to do.'

With that, she spun on her four back legs and marched down the hallway towards reception with the rest of us following behind like an angry, dishevelled army.

'OI! FUNGUS FACE!' Nancy hollered as we entered the vine-covered reception hall.

Maudlin Maloney had strung up a rope between the lepre-caravan and the staircase, and was hanging out laundry. She looked up and grinned a wonky grin at us all.

'Come to apologise to manky old Maloney, have we?'

Mum stepped forward, brandishing a mop she'd picked up from the cleaning cupboard on our way down the hall. 'It's you who needs to say sorry to us!'

'Me?' Maudlin laughed. 'You must be brain-bonked! I've never said sorry in me whole whoppsy life. What do I have to be snivellish and sorry about?'

'EVERYTHING!' yelled Dad. 'You've caused trouble from the moment you got here!' he continued. 'You cursed our guests—'

'And called us disgusterous!' Orfis added.

'You've covered our reception in a thorn briar and tried to kill us at our Trogmanay feast!' Dad snapped.

'I did no such thing!' grunted Maudlin.

'Yes, you did!' I shouted. I was too angry to care about being scared of the rancid leprechaun any more. 'The gnomad warned me you were going to do something terrible.'

'Learn to listen, quarterling,' Maudlin said to me in a discomfortingly calm voice.

'What?'

'I heard what it told you. It said you were in danger, but not what you were in danger from. You made the rest up yourself and blamed poor old Maloney!'

'Don't listen to her, Frankie!' Zingri hollered from the crowd.

'Stop it!!' I yelled. The old leprechaun was just trying to confuse us all. 'You sent your shrunken heads to gobble us up!'

'I WHAT?!' For a second Maudlin Maloney looked genuinely shocked. She glanced down at her belt and scrabbled at where the grizzly bad-luck charms had been hanging earlier. 'Where are me charms?'

'You know where there are … or were…' Nancy said, wedging her fists on her hips. 'But your little trick didn't work! Your stomach-turning trinkets have been blown to smitheroons!'

'AUNT INFLUENZA!' Maudlin shrieked. 'What have you done, you brain-boogled **EEJITS?'**

'Don't pretend you don't know exactly what happened in the dining room,' Dad said.

'You're not fooling us,' Mum added.

'I hexed your trog hog!' Maudlin said. 'I made your minkle-meat taste like dryad droppings…'

'THEN YOU TRIED TO KILL UTH!' the Molar Sisters lisped.

'I did no such thing!' the leprechaun hissed.

Was it me or was there smoke wisping out of her ears?

'That's it!' Nancy snapped. She grabbed Maudlin by the scruff of the neck and pushed her inside the little caravan. 'It's time you had a good, long think about what you've done, you rambunking rudeling.'

Then, with arms and legs moving at a terrific speed, Nancy wrapped the leprechaun's entire home with layer after layer of web, until it looked more like a ball of yarn than someone's home. The chickens clucked and cooed in alarm, but Nancy was a skilled weaver and made sure not to snag a single one of them as she wove.

'It'll take you a wee while to get out of that one!' Nancy shouted through the web-covered front door. 'Give us a yell when you're ready to say sorry.'

The tiny letterbox on the front door of the caravan flapped up between the strands of silken web.

'NEVER!' Maudlin bellowed through the narrow slot.

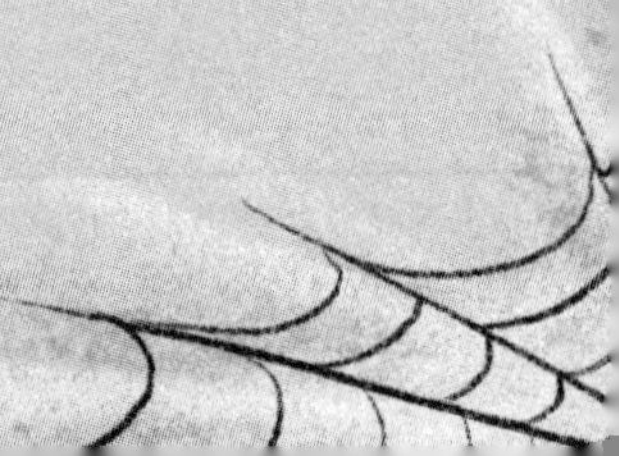

BEDTIME

'What do you think it's like?' Zingri asked in the darkness from the other side of the room.

'What?' I said.

'Being swallowed alive?'

'Dark,' I said after a while. A judder crept up my spine as the thought of it made my skin crawl.

'And smelly,' Zingri added. 'I bet the inside of a shrunken head would be super stinksome.'

'Mmm-hmm...' The clock on my bedroom wall had stopped working months ago, but I knew it must be extremely late. There was no way I was going to be feeling sleepy any time soon though, that was for sure.

After Nancy had trapped Maudlin in her caravan,

everyone had eventually shuffled off to bed. Mum had tried her hardest to keep the Trogmanay cheer going, suggesting trog nog and jiggle-dancing out on the patio, but no one really felt like it. It's amazing how having your trolliday feast wrecked by colossal dead heads can spoil the party atmosphere.

'It's lucky no one was hurt,' Zingri said. 'Or chewed!'

'Yep,' I said. I couldn't stop thinking about the gnomad's warning. What if it wasn't talking about the shrunken heads attacking our Trogmanay feast? What if there was worse to come?

'Pfffffft!' A flicker of flame burst into view in the fireplace and Hoggit puffed a few tiny fireballs across the room, lighting the candles on the windowsill and the shelf above my bed. 'Groaaarrrr!'

My pygmy soot-dragon uncurled himself from the grate, then scampered over to the bed and jumped on, wagging his tail.

'Sorry, boy,' I said, giving him a scratch under his chin. 'Are we keeping you awake?'

I looked across the room and saw Zingri's face

peering out of the folds of her hammock. She'd strung it up between the bookcase and the cupboard door, and it swayed gently from side to side as she wriggled to sit up.

'Is that sort of thing normal around here?' Zingri asked. She flopped one leg out of her swinging bed, followed by the other, then came to sit on the end of the duvet near my feet.

'Is what normal?' I said.

'Getting gobbled up like a lump of leftovers?' Zingri grinned and I could see she was just as awake as I was. 'I heard that wrinklish mermaid in the starfish bikini...'

'Berol Dunch?'

'That's the one,' Zingri said. 'When we were out in the garden earlier today, I heard her gossiping with the werepoodle.'

'Gladys Potts.'

'They were talking about someone else getting eaten up just a few weeks ago at the hotel.'

'Someone did,' I said. 'A goblin prince…'

'A GOBLIN PRINCE?!' Zingri rubbed her hands together with excitement. 'That's even better than us regular magicals nearly getting gobbled at dinner!'

'He walked into Mrs Venus's mouth by accident, when he was on the run from Squall Goblin pirates,' I said.

'SQUALL GOBLINS?!' Zingri's jaw dropped open so wide, it practically clattered across floor, and I knew I was going to have to tell her all about it … plus, I didn't want to miss out on the chance to talk about meeting my hero, CAPTAIN CALAMITUS PLANK!

'Lummy!' Zingri wriggled down under the covers and got comfy opposite me, then I told her the entire messy story about Prince Grogbah, and the curse of the diamond dentures, and Tempestra Plank, and the box full of bones, and meeting Captain Plank (Tempestra's dad), and the swash-bungling battle, and Mrs Venus falling asleep with her mouth open again, and the horrible, bone-crunching moment Prince Grogbah got grunched.

'And what was the last thing he said?' Zingri asked with wide eyes. 'Was it "AAAAAAGH!"?'

'I think he screamed, "NEVER!" when we told him to come back out,' I said, pulling a face at the horrible memory. 'The dooky little dollop refused to listen and…' I shrugged, then mimed teeth crunching together with my hands.

'That's the best story I've ever heard!' Zingri looked up at the poster of Calamitus Plank on the wall and laughed. 'I can't believe we missed all the action.'

'We were cursed and nearly got eaten today!' I said, throwing a pillow at Zingri. 'That's a lot of action too!'

'I know,' she giggled, 'but a swash-bungling battle

with a skeleton would be even better. I've never had one of those before!'

'Wait till you see this,' I said and hopped out of bed. I shuffled quickly over to a small gold box on the shelf above the fireplace. The snow and ice from the reception hall hadn't reached all the way up to my secret bedroom above the library, but it was still freezing cold.

I grabbed the gold box and darted back to the bed.

'What is it?' Zingri asked, trying to get a better look at what was in my hand.

'This,' I said, yanking the blankets over my legs, then holding the box up to the candlelight, 'is the coolest thing of all!'

I opened the gold box mega-slowly for extra-dramatic effect, then pulled out the diamond tooth that Calamitus gave to me after we won the battle and defeated Grogbah.

'Ta-dah!'

It sparkled and twinkled in the darkness, reflecting tiny stars all over the walls and ceiling.

Dad had looped some string round the glittering tooth's roots, so I could wear it round my neck whenever I wanted.

'What is it?' Zingri asked again. 'It looks like…'

'It's one of THE ACTUAL diamond dentures!'

'NO WAY!' Zingri gasped, making a grab for it.

'It's true!' I said and put the loop of string round my neck. 'It's magical. The dentures helped bring Captain Plank back from the dead. He was just a pile of bones before he got his knobbly hands on them again.'

'That was the whole set of teeth though,' Zingri grunted, trying to look unimpressed. 'Just one tooth isn't very magical.'

I stuck my tongue out at my yeti friend and she laughed.

'I suppose so,' I said. 'But I still think it's pretty terrific.'

'Definitely,' said Zingri, nodding. 'We should build a snowgoblin tomorrow and stick the tooth in its mouth!'

'What?' I said. 'Why?'

'It might come alive!' Zingri chuckled. 'We could have a snow-servant to bring us trog nog and earwax crackers for the rest of the trolliday!'

'Haha!' I blurted. 'Maybe you're ri—'

I was silenced by the sound of Hoggit growling. I looked down and saw the red glow between my little dragon's scales had faded to a rancid green colour.

'Grrrrrrrrrrrr.'

'Are you okay, boy?' I asked and placed my hand on the top of his head. He was cold!

Pygmy soot-dragons only ever glow green when they sense terrible danger. It's one of the warning signs they use when living in packs in the wild.

'Something's wrong,' I whispered to Zingri.

'Nah!' she huffed and tossed back the pillow I'd thrown a few minutes ago. 'You're still just all bonejangled from earlier.'

Hoggit growled again. Louder this time.

'He never does this,' I said as quietly as I could. 'Not unless—'

'SHHHHH!' Zingri jolted to attention. Her eyes widened and the hair on her neck and shoulders bristled. She reached an arm across the bed and clapped her hand over my mouth.

We had both heard it.

The wallpaper was muttering again…

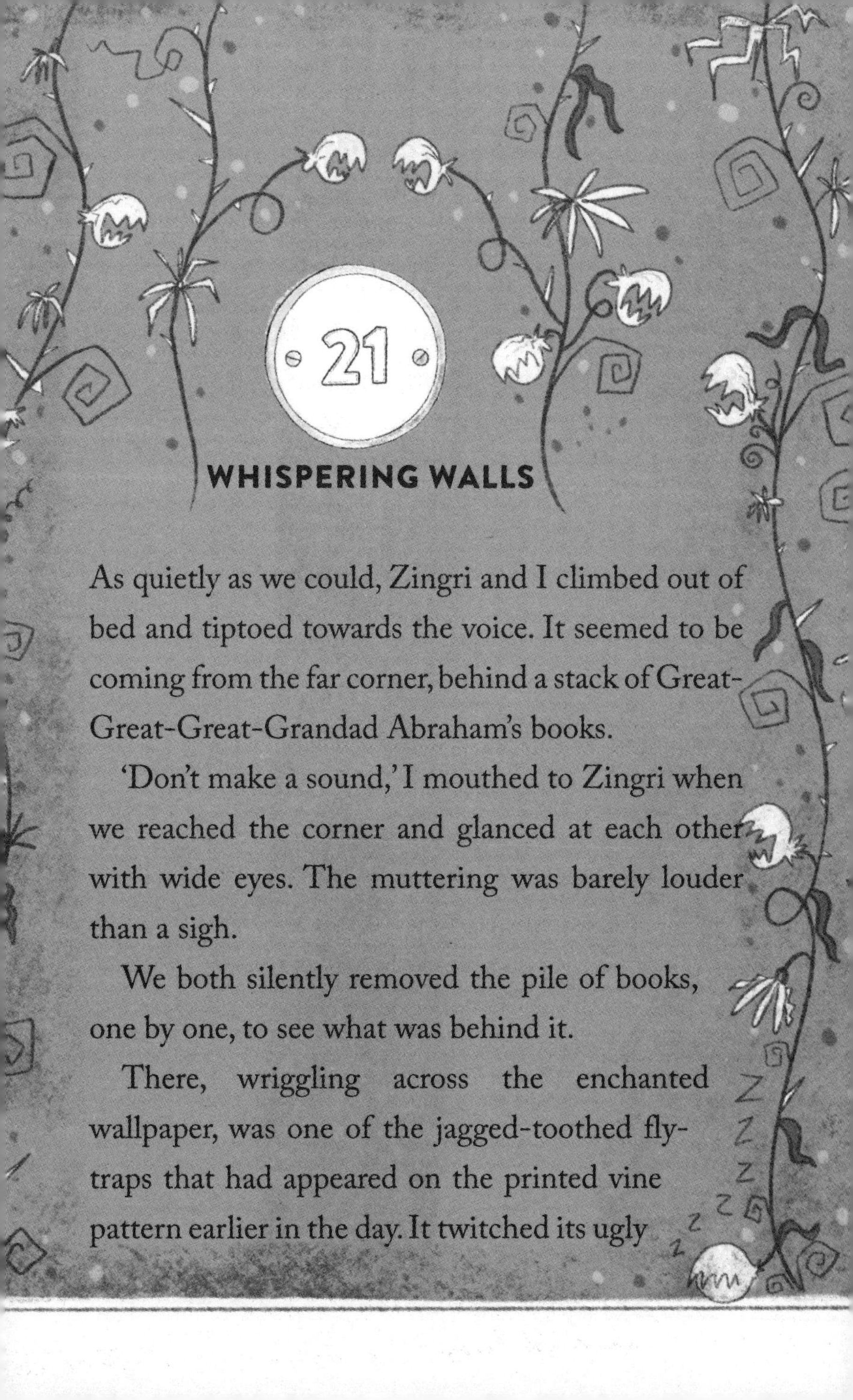

21

WHISPERING WALLS

As quietly as we could, Zingri and I climbed out of bed and tiptoed towards the voice. It seemed to be coming from the far corner, behind a stack of Great-Great-Great-Grandad Abraham's books.

'Don't make a sound,' I mouthed to Zingri when we reached the corner and glanced at each other with wide eyes. The muttering was barely louder than a sigh.

We both silently removed the pile of books, one by one, to see what was behind it.

There, wriggling across the enchanted wallpaper, was one of the jagged-toothed fly-traps that had appeared on the printed vine pattern earlier in the day. It twitched its ugly leaves, and squirmed its tendrils in such a snake-like way, it made my skin prickle with goosebumps, despite being just a drawing.

'It's wandering in the hotel,' the ghastly vine whispered. 'Sneakish and angry and plotting, it is.'

I looked up at Zingri.

'Maloney's broken loose!' I hissed.

'Stop the blighter,' the vine mumbled again. 'Stop the blighter in the blizzard ... the sneakling in the snow ... the stranger in the storm ... or the end of the hotel is...'

I held my breath, not daring to make even the tiniest of sounds.

'The end of the hotel is here ... tonight ... destroy all magicals, it plots ... and it will destroy...'

Zingri stared at me, shocked and open-mouthed.

'It will destroy all magicals ... all of them!'

SECRETS AND STRANGERS

I clicked the dial on the arm of the chair and it started to slowly judder through the floor of my bedroom.

The quiet whirring as it travelled down the track on the library wall suddenly seemed louder than gunshots and I winced at Zingri as the chair reached the ground with a bump.

'Look!' I whispered, pointing to the library doors. They were closed now and the glass in them was frosted with ice, but it was easy to make out the orange glow of a lantern and the shape of a squat person crossing reception on the other side.

'Be careful,' said Zingri quietly as we clambered

off the chair and tiptoed across the floor.

We reached the library doors and I twisted the frozen handle as slowly as I could, opening one side of them, just a crack. Then I placed my eye to the tiny gap and scanned the reception hall.

Being a human kid with troll blood in my veins means I can usually see just as well in the dark as I can during the day, but the darkness was thicker than normal, like the kind Granny Regurgita likes to fill her bedroom with. There was strange magic filling the shadows tonight and it sent a shiver up my spine.

'What can you see?' Zingri whispered in my ear.

Everything beneath the great staircase was dark except for a few slices of moonlight that glinted in from the windows on the upper landings.

'Ummm...' I looked about, searching the gloom with my troll-vision, but spotted nothing. Maloney's lepre-caravan was still wrapped tightly in a ball of Nancy's unbreakable thread with the chickens peacefully snoozing on top of it. I could see the faint glow of candles coming from inside the web-covered caravan windows and the sound of Maudlin muttering to herself. She was still in there…

'She hasn't escaped,' I mouthed to Zingri. 'Maloney's still trapped inside her home.'

'Then who did we just see?' Zingri asked. She leaned in above me and pressed her eye to the gap as well.

'I'm not sure,' I whispered, staring deeper into the darkness between the snowdrifts and snaking briars. 'Maybe the wallpaper got it wrong?'

Suddenly something fast and black sped silently through the air, glinting across the shafts of moonlight, and landing on the stone counter with a low squawk and a scattering of snow from its wings. It was the gnomad's magpie.

For a second my first thought was to call out to it, asking if it had seen anything suspicious … until it turned its head to the thickest of shadows and croaked, 'It'sss sssafe! There'sss no one here.'

Instantly the small lantern I'd spotted through the frosted glass glinted into life again and the gnomad stepped out from its hiding place beneath the stairs.

'Let'sss get thisss over with,' the magpie grumbled, clacking its talons against the hard and frosty surface of the reception counter.

My heart started racing so fast I thought it was about to play a tune on the inside of my ribs. What was going on?

'Patience, Jindabim!' said a voice I'd never heard before. It was coming from under the gnomad's clay mask. 'This needs to be done properly.'

I felt Zingri grip my shoulder with surprise. Gnomads can't talk. Everybody knows that. It's why the strange little creatures always keep an animal familiar to speak for them. This wasn't a gnomad at all!

'Let'sss teach them all a lessson,' the magpie rasped.

'Not long now, Jin,' the not-a-gnomad chuckled. It lifted the lantern and I caught a glint of green from the single eyehole of its mask. 'Revenge is close.'

With that, it reached up and pulled the clay thing from its head.

'I can't wait to sssee them sssquirm!'

the magpie cackled.

For a moment the small figure underneath the mask was obscured by the impenetrable shadows, but then it stepped into the moonlight and I found myself staring at a small pale-faced figure with jet-black hair and a patch over his right eye. He lifted his head and grinned at the bird. It was a boy… A HUMAN BOY!

I gasped a lungful of freezing winter air, and had to clap my arm across my mouth and nose to stop myself from coughing and giving away our hiding place.

'He's human!' I hissed at Zingri.

'What does he mean about revenge?' she said, looking as confused as I felt. 'What's going on, Frankie?'

I opened the door a tiny bit more and stared with wide eyes and the sound of my heartbeat thundering in my ears.

The pale-faced boy glanced up at the portrait hanging above the counter and laughed wickedly.

'There you are, you dim-witted old fool,' he jeered

at Abraham's painted face. 'I bet you didn't think you'd see me again.'

'It'sss a pity he popped hisss clonkersss,' Jindabim said with a sickening croak. 'I'd peck out hisss eyesss if he was ssstill humpling about the place.'

The boy snickered at the magpie's comment. How did they know Great-Great-Great-Grandad Abraham?

'It's time, Jindabim,' the boy said. 'Get the goblin.'

It was all happening too fast for me to take it in. Goblin? What goblin?

I watched as the magpie took off again in a flurry of feathers and swooped upwards past the spiral staircase. If I remembered correctly, Mum had booked the gnomad into one of the small rooms on the second floor.

'K-kaaawk!' it crowed as it vanished over the lip of the landing and flapped out of sight down the second-floor corridor.

I waited, trying to slow down my thoughts, as the mysterious boy scuffed about in the snow.

The bird was gone for just a moment before it

reappeared, carrying the birdcage-shaped piece of luggage it had told Dad off for touching.

'Got it!' Jindabim cackled as it came in to land, lowering the strange luggage gently onto the stone counter. 'Got the goblin!'

'Excellent,' the boy said. He reached up and untied the cloth that was tightly wrapped round the object, dropping it to the snowy ground. 'Let's see how our little friend is doing.'

LOOK WHO'S BACK!

'YOU LIARLY, FIB-MONGERING SKWONKER!'

Somehow I managed to keep from falling down while screaming and peeing my pyjamas with shock and surprise. What had looked like a birdcage-shaped piece of luggage was actually a large glass bell jar, and in it … in it was … the green, glowing ghost of…

'I'VE BEEN CRUMPED UP IN HERE ALL DAY LIKE A SARDOON IN A TINKERY-TIN!'

…Prince Grogbah!!!

The snivelling little goblin ghost wedged his tiny hands onto his hips and tapped one of his curly-toed shoes grumpily.

'Do you know who I am?' he whinged. **'MY MOOMSY IS QUEEN LATRINA!** She'd have you thrown in prison if she knew I was in here! I'm the heir to the throne of the Dark and Dooky Deep, dontcha know?!'

'Silence!' the boy said. 'We've got more important things to be getting on with.'

'Don't silence me, you squivelling little

CARBONKLE!' Grogbah jumped up and down with rage inside the glass jar. 'I'm the reason you found this place! You'd still be out there somewhere, snuffling about for clues, if I hadn't shown you the way.'

'I know!' the boy said, shooting Prince Grogbah a bad-tempered look.

'I wanted to watch them all get **GOBBLED!** You told me I could!'

'I KNOW!' the boy grunted, louder this time.

'Your mangy PARROT got to watch—'

'I'm a magpie, ssstupid!' Jindabim screeched back at the little ghost.

'Stop it, both of you!' the boy commanded in a hushed voice.

'Well, it's not **FAIR!'** Grogbah barked. 'All I wanted was to see that bratly little Frankie get **CHUNGLED UP** into porky pieces!'

The boy ignored Grogbah – he seemed to be searching the stone reception counter for something.

'Did they scream?' Grogbah asked in a quieter voice. 'As they were grunched?'

'There was lotsss of ssscreaming,' Jindabim croaked.

'HAHA!' Grogbah clapped his little hands together. 'I hope they all thought of me right before they were gobbled!'

'They didn't,' said the boy.

'Eh?' Grogbah's face twisted in horror. 'Why not?'

'They weren't gobbled!'

'WHAT?'

'The plan went wrong!' the boy snapped, spinning round to glare at Grogbah.

Grogbah's lower lip started to tremble.

'That dim-witted spider ruined everything at the last minute,' the boy huffed. He was so angry, the words almost flew out of his mouth like darts. 'The hideous leprechaun's shrunken heads were the only thing left in porky pieces after everyone de-miniaturised.'

Behind me, Zingri gasped.

'Did you hear that?' she whispered. 'Maloney was innocent all along!'

I looked over at the faint glow coming from

inside Maudlin Maloney's web-wrapped caravan and felt a rush of guilt bubbling up from my belly. We'd got it so wrong. The only thing that grizzly old leprechaun was guilty of was a few unimpressive hexes.

'And Frankie Banister wasn't squished?' Grogbah whimpered, catching my attention again. 'Not even a winksy bit?'

'No,' said Jindabim. 'Not even a tiny bit crunkled.'

'Or chomplicked?'

'NO!'

'THEN WHY HAVE YOU GOT ME LOCKED UP IN HERE?' Grogbah pounded his tiny hands on the glass and it clanged with a sharp, ghostly TING! The jar must have been enchanted or Grogbah would have stuck his arm right through it.

'WILL YOU SHUT UP?! You'll wake the whole hotel!' the boy hissed. 'You're in there because you're loud and stupid and I can't have you giving us away before we get the job done.'

'LOUD? STUPID? HOW DARE YO— What job?' Grogbah said.

'It'sss not all over yet,' Jindabim croaked.

'It's not?' cooed the little goblin ghost as a hopeful grin crept across his face.

'Not even close,' said the boy. 'There's more than one way to get rid of the Banisters.'

Grogbah giggled with glee.

'And, anyway, I've decided we need to aim higher,' the boy continued. 'Getting Frankie and his stupid family gobbled isn't enough. I want revenge on every single magical creature in this stinking hotel.'

'Really?' Grogbah asked.

'Really! We're going to break the invisibility spell that protects this place and expose them all,' the boy sneered. 'Then the humans will come with their helicopters and their tanks and blast the Nothing To See Here Hotel into a pile of rubble! The muddle-brained magicals will be locked away in zoos before they can even think about escaping.'

'But how?' Grogbah asked. 'The invisibility spell is as old as the hotel itself. It'll be a trickly-pickle to break.'

The strange child smiled at Grogbah.

'That's what you think,' he said, then placed his hands on the reception counter. For the tiniest of seconds all the twisty runes carved around its stone edges flashed the exact green of the boy's single eye. 'I've done my homework. The runes on this ugly block of rock are enchanted with troll magic. It's what keeps the hotel invisible to humans. All we have to do is crack it.'

'Well, that shouldn't be too diffidonk,' Grogbah laughed, looking impressed. 'I suppose if we could get our grabbers on a few tools, or maybe one of those hammerish thingies.'

'That would be too noisy,' the boy said. 'We'd be caught in seconds.'

'What are we going to do then?' Grogbah grumbled, pulling a moody face.

'We're going smash it in one quick crunch.' The boy pointed up to the closed sky door, ten floors above. 'We'll drop it from there!'

'Have you been brain-bonked?' the little goblin ghost scoffed. 'Who's going to do that?'

Jindabim fluttered to the boy's shoulder and the pair of them leaned menacingly towards the glass jar.

'You are,' they said to a very startled Grogbah.

'NOT SO FAST!'

Now … I didn't want to ruin the drama and excitement of discovering the gnomad was actually a seriously sinister mystery-boy plotting to destroy the hotel, and Prince Grogbah was back in all his griping glory, so I left you to it for a few pages.

And weren't they good ones?

I KNEW YOU'D AGREE!!!

So, not wanting to spoil all the tension, I waited until now to tell you that while Grogbah and his strange captor were nattering away about their dastardly plans, the wallpaper had been quietly whispering all over the hotel.

Back around the time that Grogbah yelled,

'MY MOOMSY IS QUEEN LATRINA!' I noticed a pair of faces peeking over the railing of the third-floor balcony. It was Mum and Dad.

Then, only a few seconds later, I saw Nancy sneaking a quick look round the corner of the archway that leads down to the kitchen.

Words can't even begin to explain the massive rush of relief I felt when I knew that Zingri and I weren't going to have to face this peculiar pair alone. I nearly burst out crying!!

Anyway … where were we? Ah, yes…

'Have you been brain-bonked?' the little goblin ghost scoffed. 'Who's going to do that?'

Jindabim fluttered to the boy's shoulder and the pair of them leaned menacingly towards the glass jar.

'You are,' they said to a very startled Grogbah.

'ME?' the little goblin ghost blurted. 'Not on your nelly! You must be twizzled! Are your panty-bloomers on too tight?'

'Ghosts can move things without touching them,

correct?' the boy asked.

'Well ... yes...' Grogbah mumbled. 'But that's just small things like books or shoes ... maybe twitching a few curtains or jangling the odd chain while going **"WOOOOOO!"**. I can't lift that blunking great thing!'

'Maybe not you alone,' the boy said, 'but more of you could.'

'More? How are you going to get more ghosts?'

The boy's face split into a grin that would have made a snake queasy.

'I may be human, but that doesn't mean I don't have certain ... powers.'

The boy lifted the patch that covered his right eye for a moment and a flash of green light filled the room.

'Watch!' he said. The air above reception suddenly crackled as Lady Leonora Grey and Wailing Norris materialised, but something was very wrong. They were floating limply, as still as soldiers, like they were in a trance ... and their eyes were ... their eyes were glowing green just like the boy's.

'What's wrong with them?' Grogbah sniffed, turning up his snub nose at the new ghostly company. 'Snoozling, are they? Amateurs!'

'They're under my control,' the boy said. 'They've been necromanicled.'

'Oooh, handy!' Grogbah chuckled. 'Can I do that?'

'Not unlesss you've been cursssed by a graveghassst,' Jindabim answered.

'Right,' said the boy. He waved his arms about like he was directing traffic, and the thorny vines that tangled through the snowdrifts and up the walls started to creak and move. 'Shall we get this started?'

I watched in amazed dread as a particularly spiky briar, under the boy's command, snaked up the stone counter and lifted the bell jar off the little prince.

'I'm going to enjoy this,' Grogbah said, performing a few stretches after being cooped up for so long.

Lady Leonora and Wailing Norris floated down and joined the goblin ghost at the side of the stone block.

'Up we go!' Grogbah cooed. The three ghosts held out their hands and twitched their fingers at the counter. It shuddered, then crunched noisily across the black and white tiles.

For a moment it looked like it was going to be too heavy to float, but then the enormous thing wobbled into the air, just above the snow, and…

'HOLD IT!' Mum came bounding down the staircase, three steps at a time. 'HOLD IT RIGHT THERE, YOUNG MAN!'

The boy spun round, losing concentration and his grip on Lady Lenora and Wailing Norris for a moment. The counter bumped back onto the floor.

'JUST WHAT DO YOU THINK YOU'RE DOING?'

Mum looked absolutely furious. I wasn't sure how much she would have heard of the boy's conversation from all the way up on the third-floor landing, but no one was going to meddle with the reception desk and get away with it while she was around.

'Can I help you?' Dad snapped as he

raced after Mum.

My parents strode up to the child and stood over him in that parenty type way they all do.

'I'M LOST!' the boy suddenly blubbed, throwing his arms wide like he needed to be hugged. 'Please help me. I got caught in the storm, and I can't find my parents, and I think I just saw some scary ghosts moving this block of stone!'

Ha! The creepy kid had no idea Mum and Dad had been spying on him. Even if they hadn't, lying to Mum is more difficult than scrubbing out the basement bedroom after Mr Vernon, the Stink Demon, has been to stay. She can sniff out a fib from one hundred paces.

'Oh, you poor thing!' Mum said, suddenly stopping and looking shocked. 'How on earth did you get here?'

WHAT?! I watched in astonishment as both my parents crowded round the strange boy, fussing and comforting. If I didn't think fast, Mum would be hugging the little brat in no time and he'd do something terrible to her.

There was nothing left to lose…

'WAIT!!' I screamed and dashed out through the library doors with Zingri lumbering behind me. 'HE'S LYING!'

The boy jolted his head in my direction and a determined scowl creased his forehead.

'I'm not lying!' He began to sob. 'Please. I'm so frightened. Won't you help me find my way home? I'M ALL ALONE IN THE WORLD!'

'Oh, you sweet child,' Mum said, bending down and placing an arm round his shoulder.

'STOP!' Zingri shouted.

'Get away from him!' I yelled at Mum.

Mum took the boy's hand and stood angrily up again.

'Francis Banister!' she snapped. 'What is wrong with you? And you, Zingri? Can't you see a human has wandered in from the street? We need to get him home.'

I could barely speak, I was so surprised and angry. This boy came into the hotel with a plan to destroy us all and my mother takes his word over mine? I opened my mouth to protest and then she winked.

I closed my mouth. Haha! My brilliant mum was playing this little blighter at his own game!

She looked me square in the face, then darted her eyes to something above us. Trying not to attract attention, I carefully looked upwards and saw Nancy silently creeping across the wall. She was getting in position to snare our unwelcome guest with her web.

I looked back to the boy, who was smiling sourly. He clearly thought he'd outsmarted us.

'I can't imagine how terrified you must have felt,' Mum said, shuffling the kid into the centre of the floor near the fountain. 'If you just wait here, I'll go and find—'

'WATCH OUT!!' Grogbah suddenly screamed, waggling a stumpy green finger. He'd spotted Nancy.

Mum and Dad spun round to where the little ghost was hovering by the hatstand and...

'AAAAAAAAGH!!' Mum looked like she'd seen a ghost. Well ... I suppose she really had. It's nearly impossible to spot ghosts from a distance, they just look like smoke, so, from their hiding place on the third-floor balcony, my parents had missed the return of Grogbah.

'YOU?' Dad yelped, pointing in disbelief at the curly-shoed spectre.

'PRINCE GROGBAH? HOW?' Mum squawked.

'I'M BACK, YOU DISGUSTING BANISTUMPS! NOW YOU'RE IN FOR IT!' Grogbah shrieked back at them. **'SEIZE THEM, OCULUS!'**

For a second nobody moved.

Who on earth was Oculus?

OCULUS NOCTURNE

THWAP!

The boy jabbed a finger in the air and hundreds of vines whipped from all directions, wrapping round our ankles and wrists.

'NO!' Mum and Dad shouted as the vines tangled round their legs and arms, forcing them down onto their knees and holding them tightly in place.

The creepers crackled and crunched as they snaked round my waist, squeezing the air out of me, then yanking me down by my parents.

I glanced over at Zingri, but she had been pinned to the staircase by the extra-spiky briar, which still clutched the bell jar in one of its twitching tendrils.

Zingri tore great chunks of vine away, but they were instantly replaced with more strangling tendrils.

'HOW DARE YOU!' the boy screeched. His face turned pink and his eye was practically bulging with rage. 'FOOLISH, LOATHSOME MAGICALS!'

He jabbed his finger towards Nancy this time and she was catapulted off the wall, then instantly wrapped in a net of thorns above our heads.

'Oh, my darlings!' Nancy wailed down to us as the briar carried her higher and higher until she was dangling among the chandeliers. 'I'm sorry! I wasn't quick enough!'

'Silence!' the boy yelled. 'All of you!'

'You can't order us around in our own hotel!' Dad bellowed back, struggling against the vines. 'Let us go!'

'Lady Leonora! Wailing Norris!' Mum shouted to our ghost guests, who seemed to be fast asleep in mid-air. 'Raise the alarm! Wake the hotel!'

'Nice try,' said the boy, grinning. 'Your spook friends work for me now.'

'You can't do this!' Dad hollered. 'Just who do you think you are?'

The boy crunched carefully across the snow towards us.

'The question is not who do I think I am,' he said to Dad, 'but who do YOU think I am?' He looked from Dad, to Mum, and back to Dad. 'Well?'

'I think you're a very rude little boy!' Mum snapped. 'Your parents will be furious when they find out what you've been up to!'

'My parents are long gone,' the crazy child said through gritted teeth. 'And I'm not a little boy!'

'That's exactly what you are!' Dad said. 'A naughty little boy … with powers, maybe, but a little boy nonetheless.'

'I AM ONE HUNDRED AND TWENTY-SEVEN YEARS OLD!'

'And three-quarters!' Grogbah added.

Nobody spoke. This was all SO confusing. The boy didn't look a day older than me.

'I am very old indeed and much wiser than all of you,' he said. 'And very dangerous too!' Then he laughed the kind of howling laugh that only a super-scary villain-type person would do.

He turned to me and smiled.

'Come on, Frankie. Aren't you going to say hello? Don't you know who I am?'

'Yeah … don't you know who he is, you bonce-belching skrunt?' Grogbah joined in.

I stared at the boy and wracked my brains. Something about his face did seem familiar, but I couldn't put my finger on it.

'Tell him, **TELL HIM, TELL HIM!'** Grogbah said, clapping his hands and interrupting my thoughts. 'They're going to boogle their bunions with shock!'

'I'm your great-great-uncle, Oculus.'

I gasped. My uncle…? Suddenly I realised who this person was. THAT FACE!?! It was one I had looked at almost every day of my life. How could I not have recognised him?

Standing in the middle of our reception hall was the boy from the painting of Great-Great-Great-Grandad Abraham. I had stared at him for hours

at a time, wondering who he could be, and now he was here. Apart from the patch over his right eye, he looked exactly the same!

My head started swimming with questions, and I remembered Maudlin Maloney's words: 'I knew old Abe well in me earlier years … and his son…'

'W-w-what did you say?' asked Dad, looking just as shaken as me.

'I should have known you stinking halflings and quarterlings would be too stupid to spot it. It's funny really! My portrait has been hanging in the

hotel for over a hundred years and you didn't have a clue who I was until I told you. I don't know why I bothered wearing a disguise.'

The boy kicked the clay gnomad mask that had been discarded in the snow.

'Uncle Oculus?' I stammered. The hairs on the back of my neck stood on end at the sound of it. What if Maudlin Maloney had been right? 'B-b-but I don't have a Great-Great-Uncle Oculus.'

'Oh, yes, you do.' He bowed. 'Oculus Nocturne. Surprise!'

'There's

been no one of that name in the Glump/Banister family tree. Ever!' said Mum.

'You are mistaken,' Oculus said.

'There's no Oculus Nocturne in our family tree! I should know. I have to dust it!' Dad shouted. He was losing his patience.

'Jindabim!' Oculus barked and his magpie whirled into the air from its perch on the water-witch fountain's hand.

We watched as it flew towards the enormous tapestry that hung on the wall at the base of the staircase. It was a great moth-eaten old thing that Mum hated, and on its threadbare surface was woven an ornate family tree with the names of every member. At the bottom my name was stitched in bright colours with Mum's and Dad's just above. But the higher up you went, the more faded and tatty the names became …

'K-KAAAWK!' Jindabim crowed as he skimmed the floor, then soared vertically up the front of the tapestry. I read the names as the magpie flew past them … Mankle Banister, Stodger Banister,

Bombastis Banister, Festus McGurk, Lylifa Glump, Crumpetra Glump, Blundus Banister, Limina Lightfoot, Grizhilda Glump, Grottle Glump, Rozomastrus Bracegirdle, Zennifer Glump, Regurgita Glump, Abraham Banister, …

Jindabim pecked at a loose thread just next to Grandad Abe's name and pulled hard, flapping away from the tapestry. I watched with a pounding heart and a sinking feeling in my belly as the thread unravelled from the weave, uncovering two names that had been completely sewn over. One was a woman's name, Olympia Nocturne, and the other was my Great-Great-Uncle Oculus!

A GRAVE CHILD

There was silence for what seemed like a squillion years.

I could see Oculus was enjoying the bewildered expressions on our faces. He laughed spitefully at us as Jindabim swooped back down and landed on his arm, the long strand of thread dangling from either side of its beak.

'I don't understand…'

It was Dad who finally spoke, still wrestling with the clutching vines. 'Why have I never heard of you? And why do you still look like a boy?'

Oculus glanced over to a smirking Grogbah and rolled his eyes.

'I think the halfling is asking for a bedtime story,'

he snickered.

'Ooooh, lummy!' Grogbah said. 'Tell it to them, just like you told me. Don't miss out any of the disgusterous parts.'

'I promise,' Oculus leered. He waved his hand and a knot of vines creaked up through the snow, forming a small throne. Then he sat down like some tiny ruler about to speak to his kingdom and began.

'I bet you think you know all about dear old Abraham Banister, don't you?'

'Of course,' said Dad.

'He was a world-famous explorer,' I said.

'WRONG!' Oculus barked at me. 'Abraham Banister was assistant to my mother, Olympia Nocturne. She was the greatest explorer who ever lived! Fighting her way across deserts and through the deepest, darkest jungles, she discovered some of the most precious treasures and strange species of animals known to man. All Abraham Banister did was carry her suitcases.'

'That's a lie!' Dad yelled, struggling to free himself.

'I'm afraid it's not,' said Oculus. 'He was a snivelling coward.'

'A grunting little gonker!' Grogbah cooed with delight.

'He and my mother were in love and they travelled the world, Mum doing all the dangerous adventuring and Abraham making cups of tea.' Oculus's face twisted into a grimace at the sound of Abe's name. 'Eventually I was born and for a little while we were a happy family. It wasn't until one terrible night when I was eight years old that Abraham showed just how lily-livered he was.'

'What do you mean?' I asked.

'We were in India, searching for a lost shrine, when we accidentally disturbed a graveghast bathing in the River Ganges under the light of the full moon. The grotesque fairy was so furious, she

laid a dire spell on us there and then. Mother was turned into a bloated toad and fell into the rushing water. She was never seen again. I, on the other hand, was cursed with the graveghast's kiss.'

'That doesn't sound so bad—' Mum began.

'When a death fairy blows its kiss at a human, they are doomed to walk the earth for ever and ever!'

'Ahh,' said Mum. 'That's not so good,'

'My heart pumps dust around my veins and I've been stuck like this for over a hundred years, neither living nor dead, always cold and miserable, incapable of sleep! And we don't stay fresh, you know.' Oculus tapped his eyepatch. 'Bits fall off!'

'Right,' Dad suddenly chirped before the strange boy could say anything else. 'Thank you for the fascinating story, Oculus. It really was lovely. Now, if you could just make these vines go away, I'm sure we could sit down over a nice pot of tea and discuss this like—'

'I'M NOT FINISHED!' Oculus bellowed in Dad's face. He took a deep breath and quietly continued. 'The only person who managed to escape being cursed by the graveghast was … you guessed it … Abraham Banister. He ran away the second he saw that dreadful creature rising out of the river. He abandoned us, scampering back to England and claiming all my mother's wonderful discoveries as his own.'

I felt sick listening to my great-great-uncle's story. It was heartbreaking. How could Grandad Abe have done something so awful?

'I discovered Abe had come to live in Brighton because of some old newspaper reports I found years later, boasting about his adventures. I was too late, however. By the time I knew where he was, Daddy-dearest had already married a revolting magical and vanished behind the invisibility spell. I spent the past century searching for this freakish hotel, but even my new powers couldn't help me. I was still human after all…'

'Then how did you get here?' Mum asked angrily. 'Why now?'

'My stroke of luck came when an angry little

goblin ghost sensed my presence nearby—'

'That's me!' Grogbah interrupted, giving a little wave.

'With Prince Grogbah's help and the added bonus of a magical blizzard pointing the way, I've finally found you.'

Oculus stood up, calmly straightening out a crease in his shirt. 'And now I'm going to expose the hotel to the human world!'

NOT LONG NOW…

Right, we're nearly there, my human friend.

THE GRAND FINALE!

I know there's no way in a month of Mondays you imagined that all the trouble earlier in the day was caused by a long-lost human relative dressed up as a gnomad. I certainly didn't.

And now you'll be desperately wondering what happened next and I can't say I blame you.

What with me, Mum, Dad and Zingri shackled by vines, and Nancy being turned into a spider-chandelier, dangling above us, it was all looking pretty grim.

Having Grogbah's griping little ghost back didn't

help, and my insane child-uncle about to smash the rune-covered stone that kept the hotel invisible was the final cherry on the cockroach cake.

I admit it all sounds incredibly hopeless, but you don't think we went down without a fight do you?

Ready?

A FAMILY FEUD

Oculus hopped onto the stone block, then clicked his fingers and smiled as his ghost servants sprang back into action. Grogbah joined Lady Leonora and Wailing Norris at the sides of the counter and they all stretched their twitching fingers towards it.

'Up we go!' Oculus said, then turned and grinned at us as they all started to rise into the air.

I looked at my parents, who were still struggling against the strangling creepers. There was no way we were going to wriggle free without help.

'YOU CAN'T DO THIS, YOU WEE ROTTER!' Nancy shrieked as Oculus rode the counter higher and higher. She wasn't having any luck either. Her arms and legs were flailing this way and that, but the vines held her tightly and didn't let go. 'SOMEBODY STOP HIM!'

It was Zingri who answered Nancy's plea.

I nearly jumped out of my skin with surprise as the yeti girl let rip with the rumbliest roar I'd ever heard.

No. I'm not telling it right. It wasn't a roar … the noise coming out of her mouth was more like she was singing a low and extremely loud **HOOOOOOOG!** It echoed off the walls and rattled the icicles that hung from every surface. Lumps of ice started falling in all directions and smashing on the snowy floor.

'HOOOOOOOG!!!'

When she finally ran out of breath and ended the long note, everyone was staring at her. Even Oculus and the ghosts had stopped floating upwards and were gawping down, frozen in mid-air.

'Ha!' Oculus laughed, pulling a mocking face. 'Was that supposed to save you? It'll take more than some ugly singing, you mangy fleabag.'

'I wasn't singing!' Zingri said with a mischievous

wink. 'That was Ulkish.'

'What?' Oculus said. He opened his mouth to say more, but was silenced by the sound of thundering hooves.

'YOU AIN'T SEEN NOTHING YETI!' Zingri howled.

CRAAAAAAAAAAAAAAAAAAASSHH!!

Before anyone had time to dive out of the way, the Arctic ulk exploded through the archway leading to the kitchen. Its enormous antlers were too wide to fit through the gap and they tore huge clumps of stone and brick down from either side.

'HOOOOOOOOOOOOOOOG!' the ulk bellowed as clouds of steam rose into the air from its flared nostrils. **'HOOOOOOOOOOOOOOOG!'**

'The caravan!' Zingri shouted to the colossal creature, waving and pointing her free arm at Maudlin Maloney's little home. 'Break it open!'

'HOOOOOOOOOOOOOOOG!' The Arctic ulk lumbered over to the little wooden hut on wheels and swiftly ripped the front wall off with one swish of its antler. Splintered wood and torn spider's web tumbled onto the floor, as Maudlin's terrified chickens squawked and flapped about.

Inside, a wide-eyed leprechaun wearing a flannel nightdress and a filthy mob cap shrieked in shock from her little bed.

'WHAT THE BLUNKERS IS OCCURRINATIN'?!' the ancient fairy hollered, clutching the bedsheets to her chest. She stumbled out of bed and ran to where her door had been only moments ago. 'Me home! What's the meanin' of this, you rambunkin' little runties? First I'm locked up like a prisony-prawn and now me door's been boogled!'

'Maudlin!' I shouted. 'I'm sorry! We know it wasn't you who ruined the feast!'

'I told you that all along, you ninkumplumper!' she bawled back at me.

'I know! I was wrong! Please help us!' I pleaded.

'Help?' she said, her face creasing up with confusion. 'Help how? Why are you all bundled up like that?'

'It's him!' Zingri yelled, pointing at the floating stone block and the boy standing on top of it.

Maudlin looked up and gasped at the sight.

'A human!' she grunted. 'I knew some tricksy-trevor was skulkin' about the hotel … but not **A HUMAN!'**

Oculus, who'd been staring down at the chaos below with an open mouth, suddenly jolted. He glared at the three ghosts floating beside him.

'Hurry!' he ordered. 'Higher, you idiots!'

The ghosts began twitching their fingers and they all started to rise again.

'He's going to smash the stone!' Dad cried to the leprechaun. 'It has the invisibility spells on it!'

'We'll be discovered!' Mum joined in.

Maloney's face twisted into a grimace of anger. She glowered up at my great-great-uncle and balled her gnarled hands into fists.

'SO!' she cackled. 'You want to play with the big blighters, do you? **NO HUMAN'S GOIN' TO TRUMPLE MAGICALS WHILE MANKY OLD MALONEY'S AROUND!'** Then she leaned out of the huge hole in her caravan and hollered, **'GIRLS!!!!!'**

All at once, Maudlin's squadron of flying chickens

flapped onto the rusted roof of their mistress's home and snatched up whatever strings of web they could get their claws on.

'Fly, ladies! **FLY!**' Maloney screeched.

As the caravan wobbled into the air, she darted back inside for a moment, then reappeared, waving a strange-looking object above her head.

'Here!' she shouted, throwing it to the snowy ground at my feet. 'Even a bad-luck fairy keeps a few lucky knick-knacks, you know!'

I looked down and saw a knot of silvery weeds wrapped in a green ribbon with lots of little ornaments and shells hanging off it.

'What's that?' I shouted. Whatever it was, it didn't look very useful.

'Trinkle-thistles!' Maudlin replied as the caravan bounced off the staircase, nearly sending her sprawling back to earth. 'They're good for tummy aches, trapped wind, and reversing darklish spells. Very handy!'

We all stared at the bunch of weeds, desperately willing it to do something.

CRACK! CRICK! CRUNCH!

Suddenly the vines that bound us and covered most of the reception hall disintegrated to dust in one small pop! My arms and legs were instantly freed and I nearly toppled face first into Mum and Dad.

All around, tatty bits of old creeper rained down and vanished into the snow, followed by a flailing Nancy. She tumbled to the ground with a painful **UNHHHH,** sending a flurry of frost into the air.

'Quick!' Zingri yelled from the base of the staircase. 'GET HIM!'

That was it! In an instant, we were all clattering up the stairs, trying to catch up with Maudlin's caravan and the floating block of stone high above.

'Don't let him reach the sky door!' Nancy huffed as she raced ahead of us. She'd given up using the stairs and was now clambering from banister to banister, jumping whole floors at a time.

I ran so fast, my lungs felt like they were burning.

Up and round the corner…

Up and round the corner…

Up and round the corner…

As Zingri and I passed the open corridors that led away from each landing, I could see frightened faces peering out from bedroom doors.

'Wath goin' on?' the Molar Sisters called to us as I raced past. 'Ith it time for breakfatht?'

'It's no use!' I heard Oculus laugh high above. I glanced up and saw that he and the ghosts had nearly reached the ceiling. 'GIVE UP, YOU WORMS!'

'Not so fast, you wee jobby!' Nancy was gaining on the insane man-boy and I watched as she vanished over the lip of the tenth-floor balcony. She'd made it!

Come on, Nancy! I thought to myself as I struggled up another flight of steps. I was only on the sixth floor.

'Abandon hope!' I heard Oculus bellow. His voice sounded high-pitched and hysterical.

'Stop!' Nancy's voice replied.

I kept running, but I still had a long way to go. I wished I could see what was happening up there.

That was the moment Nancy screamed.

There was the sound of a commotion, followed by a fast-paced thumping as something started tumbling down the stairs.

'Oh, no, you don't!' I heard Nancy grunt.

Glancing up again, I gasped as our spider-chef clattered round the bend of the stairs, rolling and banging and yelping towards me. She swung her arms this way and that, punching and kicking as great sheets of wallpaper yanked themselves off the walls and tangled round her legs.

Oculus may not have been able to stop the vine patterns from gossiping, but he could certainly control their movements.

'Watch out!' Nancy shouted. I pressed myself against the wall and narrowly missed being squashed as she thundered past.

I watched with my heart in my throat as Nancy rounded the next bend of the staircase on the floor below.

Mum and Dad, who were way behind me and Zingri, squealed in fright when they saw her crashing towards them.

'Aaaaarrrgh!' Mum grabbed Dad by the collar of his shirt and yanked him into one of the side corridors just in time.

'Don't stop now!' Zingri huffed, pulling me by the arm. 'There's still a chance!'

The pair of us continued to sprint up the stairs. With Nancy now battling more and more rolls of wallpaper as they whipped through the air, our next hope was Maudlin. She was below us now, but her chickens were flapping so frantically, they were catching up fast.

'Almost there,' Zingri said, dragging me up the last flight of stairs.

As I looked up over the tenth-floor landing, I saw that my great-great-uncle had hopped off the stone block and was now enjoying the whole spectacle from the safety of the balcony.

'You can almost smell it,' he said, sensing us standing behind him. He had his hands folded behind his back and seemed strangely calm as he watched the ghosts reach the ceiling.

'Smell what?' Zingri hissed at his back.

Oculus twisted his head and fixed us with his stare. He'd removed his eye patch and the brilliant green glow from his right socket shone on us like a searchlight.

'The end,' he said with a crooked leer.

WAKE THE WITCH

'AAAAAEEEEEEEEEEEEE!' Maudlin's lepre-caravan and her cloud of chickens suddenly burst into view over the edge of the tenth-floor balcony. She was wild-eyed, standing in the gap where her front door used to be, and in her hands she was holding some sort of wooden chest.

'Take that!' She reached inside the box, plucked out a bad-luck charm and threw it at Oculus, but it hit the banister instead. All at once the wooden railing erupted with sore-looking boils and pimples.

'How about this, then?' The leprechaun lobbed another, and another, and another. 'No human messes with magicals and gets away with it!'

'Her aim's not very good!' Zingri moaned as more and more unlucky trinkets missed their target.

In no time, the carpet had turned to mould, there was a chandelier that had broken out in a fit of sobbing, and a sofa at the end of the landing had developed a runny nose.

Oculus didn't even flinch as the bad-luck charms rained down around him. He stood, unmoving, staring up at the ghosts and the stone block. Whatever that graveghast had done to him all those years ago, it had made him fantastically powerful.

'SO!' he suddenly shouted. 'After a century of waiting, I will have revenge on my pathetic father's disgusting new family and all magicals everywhere!'

He lifted a hand to the ghosts, and was just about to give the signal for them to drop their heavy cargo, when…

''Ere, what's all this hollerin' and ruckslushing?'

I glanced over the balcony to see Orfis and Unga wandering through the broken archway, ten floors below, rubbing sleep from their eyes.

'OH, DOOKIE DROPS!' Unga blurted when

she took in the crazy scene unfolding before her.

Nancy was now charging up and down the walls, caught in a whirlwind of paper. 'Hello, dears!' she called to the yetis as she tore great strips of the stuff from around her ankles. 'A spot of help would be honkhumptious just about now!'

'Blimeybumps!' Orfis gasped as the Arctic ulk clattered past, bucking this way and that to avoid Jindabim's swooping pecks.

'MOOMA! DOODA! WE'RE UP HERE!' Zingri shouted.

Her parents ran to the centre of the reception hall and looked up.

'Oh! Giddy my gizzards!' Unga yelled when she saw us. 'What's all this, then?'

'I can't explain now!' Zingri answered. 'Help!'

'FRANKIE!' Mum's voice shouted from somewhere much lower on the staircase. 'Don't let him drop the stone!'

I looked at Zingri and could tell she was having the same thought I was. By the time Orfis and Unga made it up all the stairs, the stone counter would be in pieces on the reception floor and the hotel's invisibility spell would be broken. It was down to us now.

We both lunged towards Oculus, but we were out of time.

'DROP IT!' he screamed as we lurched forward. He clapped his hands together in front of his face and green sparks flew out from between his fingers. Suddenly, and without warning, the three ghosts vanished in a great burst of ectoplasm and…

THE STONE FELL!

The next few moments all happened in such a crazy jumble, it feels like a strange dream remembering them.

'WAIT!' Zingri screamed as the stone plunged downwards. She raced over to where Oculus was standing in the centre of the landing and, before she even realised what she was doing, Zingri booted him straight over the railing. 'YOU SKRONKER!'

The boy was flung into the air, spinning and thrashing in fear and alarm.

'NOOOOO!' In a fraction of a second, he was

plummeting down through the spiral staircase right next to the carved stone he was so intent on smashing.

'Hold it!' Maudlin shrieked above all the noise. She had ducked inside her home, but reappeared at the missing door, this time clutching a tatty old mop. **'I DON'T THINK SO!'**

The ancient leprechaun jabbed the mop in the direction of the falling boy and lump of stone. A gust of sulphur-stinking orange smoke billowed from the disgustingly stained mop-head and … and … suddenly they weren't falling any more.

'Haha!' Maudlin cackled. 'I knew this time-tinkerin' charm would come in useful one day.'

Zingri and I peered over the banister and both gawked at the bizarre view.

Oculus hadn't frozen in time completely. Both he and the counter were still falling, but it was like they were sinking through treacle at such a slow pace, it was barely possible to notice them moving.

'What now?' Zingri wheezed.

'Now you think of somethin' quick sharp!'

Maudlin replied. 'Hurry! The charm doesn't last too long! It's a very old mop! You'll have a broken invisibility spell and a very splattered little boy in a minute or two.'

I glanced at Orfis and Unga, hoping to suddenly come up with a brilliant plan, but it was no use. Even with their great yeti size, Zingri's parents couldn't catch a block of stone as big as the reception counter. It would squash them flat for sure.

That's when Zingri did something I wasn't expecting.

'The fountain!' she gasped at me.

'What?'

'The fountain, Frankie! And the diamond denture!'

'I don't understand' I said. My head felt like someone had reached inside it and set off a bunch of fireworks.

'Wake the water witch!'

'Why?'

'If she can soak that little blighter, we can freeze him with our storm jar! The desk too! That'll stop it from smashing.'

My hand touched the glittering tooth that hung around my neck.

Zingri was right! We stared at each other for a split-second, but it was all we needed. I knew I trusted her and she trusted me.

Without saying a word, Zingri picked me up.

'Orfis! Unga!' I shouted as my yeti friend lifted me over her head. 'CATCH!'

FROZEN

Zingri launched me over the edge of the balcony like a human dart.

'HAHA!' I heard Maudlin Maloney squeal as I whizzed past her caravan. **'GO GET 'EM, BOY!'**

'OH, BLUNKERS!' Mum and Dad howled from the stairs.

I nosedived towards the ground, narrowly missing my time-tinkered great-great-uncle in mid-air and praying that our yeti guests would catch me.

My eyes streamed with tears from the icy air slicing across my face and I could hardly see as the floor and two very furry shapes rushed up to meet me.

'GO ON, ORFIS!' Unga barked at her husband.

'GRAB THE LITTLE LUMPLING!'

Just as I was preparing to be smashed to smitheroons, a pair of enormous, hairy arms wrapped round me and I came to an abrupt and very winded stop.

'GOT 'IM!' Orfis beamed, putting me down gently and ruffling my hair with one of his spade-sized hands.

'Oooh, thank my lucky stumps!' Unga said with an enormous grin. 'For a second there, Frankie, I thought you were about to be pulped into porridge!'

I opened my eyes and the ground floor came swimming into focus.

'I ... I...' I stammered.

'What's he saying?' Orfis asked.

'I need...'

'Need what, my dunklet?' Unga said, leaning forward like she was about to examine me. 'Are you hungry? Thirsty? Do you need to visit the loo-loo-room?'

'GET ON WITH IT, BOY!' Maudlin's voice yelled

from above, jarring me back to my senses.

'I need to see the water witch!'

Orfis and Unga looked confused. Then they slowly pointed to the fountain in the centre of reception.

'She's just there,' Orfis said. 'You can see her any time.'

'Right where she's always been,' added Unga.

'No, you don't understand!' I shouted a little too loudly, making the yetis jump with surprise. 'You have to lift me up high. I've got to see her face.'

'Oh, why didn't you say so, my cuteyconk?'

Unga was much taller than Orfis, so she picked me up and carried me over to Aunt Zennifer's statue.

It was just then that Mum and Dad made it to the bottom of the staircase and raced across the black and white tiles towards us. It seemed that Oculus's wallpaper enchantment had faded now he was time-tinkered and Nancy joined us too, picking scraps of paper from out of her blueish/purplish perm.

'Francis!' Mum barked as she reached the base of the fountain. 'What's going on?'

'There's no time to explain,' I said as I neared the water witch's head. I'd never seen her face this close up before.

'It's now or never, Frankie!' Zingri shouted as she bounded down the stairs, not wanting to miss out on the action.

Carefully I lifted the loop of string over my head and tried to put the diamond denture into the statue's slightly open mouth ... but ... **IT DIDN'T FIT!**

Okay, I have something to admit to you, my reader friend. I know we're right at the end of the story and this part should be super-dramatic and amazing. I was about to wake up my long-dead great-great-aunt to battle against my not-so-dead great-great-uncle, but what was I supposed to do when the magic tooth wouldn't go in her gob?

Well, I'll tell you. I shoved the tooth up her left nostril and hoped for the best! Not quite so cool, but I had no choice!

'Frankie Banister!' Mum huffed. 'What on earth do you think you are doing!?!'

'Well, I never,' Orfis mumbled, staring at me like I was weirder than a bison in a ballgown. 'Are you feeling all right, lump?'

'The boy's been clonkered!' said Unga.

I tried my best to block out the chattering of my parents and our yeti friends. It had to work … it just HAD to!

Glaring at my Aunt Zennifer's cold, hard face, I searched for a shudder, or a twitch, or any sign of movement.

Nothing…

Nothing…

Nothing…

Then…

SHE BLINKED!

The power of only one tooth from Captain Plank's magical set of diamond dentures wasn't enough to turn her back to her normal fleshy self, but it certainly worked in giving her a little dose of life.

Everybody on the ground gasped as Aunt Zennifer, still the colour of stone and making loud cracking sounds, twisted her head and looked down at her distant relatives.

Unga put me on the rim of the fountain and I reached up, taking the statue's hand.

'Aunty!' I said, suddenly fighting back the feeling that I might burst into tears. 'You don't know me, but I'm your great-great-nephew, Frankie.'

My aunt didn't utter a word, but her black eyes fixed me with her stare and I thought I detected a glimmer of a smile at the corner of her cracking lips.

Zennifer flexed her arms and the glittering loops of frozen water left by the blizzard smashed and fell to pieces on the floor. She lifted her hands slowly, examining them with an expression of wonder as fresh trickles of water started to pour from both her palms.

'Your half-brother Oculus has returned and we

need your help to save the hotel and all the family.'

Zennifer jerked and looked at me, her face crunching into a frown.

'The time charm is fadin'!' Maudlin yelled above us. **'QUICK, FRANKIE!'**

'Has the world been scrumbled?' Unga blurted, scratching her head and looking more puzzled than ever. 'What in blasty-blazers is happenin' here?'

'Mooma, there's no time to explain!' Zingri snapped. She looked so serious and in charge that Unga just shut her mouth and nodded. 'Get the

storm jar ready and, when I say NOW, open it!'

Unga fished inside her shawl and pulled out the small glass container.

'I'm very confuserated, but I trust you, Zingri, my lump.'

'I can't hold it much longer!' Maudlin's cracked voice echoed off the walls.

I turned just in time to see the orange smoke that had been lazily drifting about the time-tinkered boy evaporate into nothing. There was a popping sound and all at once time caught up with Oculus and the stone reception counter and they both plummeted towards us.

'Please!' I begged my aunt, pointing upwards. 'THERE! DRENCH THEM!'

Zennifer needed no further encouragement. She raised her arms with a loud crackling crunch and a great geyser erupted from her hands.

I jumped back towards my family and the Kwinzis as the torrent of water burst into the air.

'Cor! Lummy!' Orfis cooed as we all huddled together and watched the remarkable scene unfold.

Zennifer's rumbling column of water rose higher and higher through the space between the spiral staircase as Oculus and the counter finally crashed down to meet it.

There was an almighty splash, and fountain water foamed and frothed and rained down in all directions.

'NOW!' Zingri screamed.

Instantly the entire reception hall vanished from view as Unga whipped off the storm-jar lid and everything became a booming, rushing whirlwind of ice and water and snow.

It was so loud, it felt like we were standing at the centre of some gargantuan white volcano, and then …

Silence.

I slowly opened one eye and gasped.

There in the centre of the enormous room, rising from the statue of my aunt, was the most beautiful ice formation I'd ever laid my eyes on. It reached up between the spiral staircase in vast loops and curves. Icicles hung in hundreds upon hundreds of delicate rows.

My eyes darted about the great frosty sculpture with shock and awe and I spotted the stone counter securely cradled on a jagged shelf of ice about halfway up.

'IT'S SAFE!' I grinned as a huge wave of relief washed over me.

I glanced higher still, taking in all the intricate detail of the ice tower, and then I saw him.

Right at the top of the swirling column, suspended inside its crystal-clear centre, my Great-Great-Uncle Oculus was frozen, arms and legs flailing as if he was still falling. The green glow from his right eye shimmered through the ice tower like stars, and there was a look of pure anger and hatred on his face.

A shiver ran up my spine and the hairs on the back of my neck stood on end and it definitely wasn't because of the cold.

ANOTHER TROGMANAY OVER

TA-DAH!

Well, there you have it.

I did warn you right back at the beginning of the book that this was one SERIOUSLY weird twenty-four hours in the Nothing to See Here Hotel … even by our standards.

It took us ages to decide what to do after poor Uncle Oculus had been frozen solid.

The sun rose not long after our giant fight and, before we knew it, all the hotel guests were shuffling around the ice column, scratching their heads and wondering what the strange new piece of art was all about. But we got it all sorted (well … Mum did) eventually.

She set Ooof to work, chipping the stone reception counter out from its frosty nest, and it was safely back in place in no time.

Then our handyogre started on the unfortunate grave child. He hammered away at the enormous tower of ice until there was only a neat cube of it left with Oculus trapped in its centre.

Now, don't forget that my great-great-uncle couldn't die. He'd been cursed with the graveghast's kiss after all.

NOPE! He was going to be stuck in there for a very long time, getting VERY bored indeed.

After one of Nancy's world-famous breakfasts of scrambled unicorn eggs on toast and mugful after mugful of shrimp-scale tea, the Kwinzis saddled up the Arctic ulk and got ready to head off on their journey back home to the Himalayas.

'It's just not long enough,' Unga sobbed into an oversized hanky. 'I'll miss you more than a chunker misses chipolatas.'

Orfis loaded the frozen boy in his block of ice

onto a small sled they'd hitched to the back of the ulk and grimaced.

'Ooooh, it's all a bit spookerific if you ask me!' he mumbled, visibly juddering. 'We'll keep him safe and snugly up on the glacier by our village. He won't be able to cause any more trouble there, so long as he stays frosty and freezy.'

And that was that. Before we had time to grumble or complain or cry, our Trogmanay Trolliday was over and our yeti friends were galloping down the garden path and over the frozen sea at the centre of a magical storm.

As I waved goodbye, I wanted to feel happy about stopping Oculus and saving the hotel from being discovered by the outside world, but I couldn't shake a weird gloopy feeling in my belly. I… well, I… I felt sorry for him. If everything my great-great-uncle had said was true, I wasn't surprised he wanted revenge! What if Great-Great-Great-Grandad Abraham really had been a big phoney?

I had some serious investigating to do… but before then, we had a mountain of clearing up to see to.

Mum put the enchanted mops to work with all the melting snow, and the Molar Sisters kindly used their magic wands to repair all the damage around reception caused by the fight, Maudlin set about fixing her lepre-caravan, Lady Leonora and Wailing Norris were whisked off to the nearest staircase where they could rest up and recover from terrible headaches and what they said were, 'REALLY STRANGE DREAMS!', and Granny Regurgita missed all of it.

HAHA! My grizzly grunion of a great-great-great-granny hates trolliday celebrations and didn't care a jot when I tried to tell her about Oculus later that day.

She'd heard it all before, I suppose? There have always been blizzards, and yetis, and talking birds, and angry 127-year-old boys, and water witches, and festive feasts, and leprechauns, and whispering wallpaper, and curses, and shrunken heads, and jars of extra-thick and spicy mango chutney, and goblin ghosts, and evil plans and lots and lots of 'right pickles'…

I did warn you that weird is normal to us Banisters, and I guess when you're a 476-year-old troll, there's always something crazier that's happened on some other occasion.

Ha!

Who's for a snowball fight before the last of it thaws in the garden?

COME ON!

ONE LAST THING…

Agh! **HANG ON!** Before you put this book down and go outside to play, there's just one skwinkly thing I have to tell you.

That night, after all the commotion was over and the sight of my frozen great-great-uncle was starting to go fuzzy in my memory, there was a bump in the dark.

I was lying in bed, quietly thinking about Great-Great-Great-Grandad Abraham and nodding slowly off when…

'Oi! Wake up, you ranciderous **SNOT-LUMPER!'**

I jolted awake and sat up. For a second I thought it was all happening again, and Nancy was calling me from the kitchen … until … I saw it. Sitting on the end of my bed, waggling his tiny, curly shoes over the edge, was Grogbah's ghost.

'**WELL,** now, what a whoppsy day!' he said with a mischievous twinkle in his eye. 'Who'd have thunkled it? I'll be needing somewhere bunglish and cozy to haunt now that deadly dratling has gone and I think your bedroom is the **PERFECTEROUS SPOT!'**

I stared with wide eyes as he plucked a ghostly chain out of the air and rattled it noisily at me.

'Woooooooo!' Grogbah moaned and yowled, between stifled chuckles. **'WOOOOOOOOOO!'**

Steven B is an award-winning children's writer, actor, voice artist and host of World Book Day's The Biggest Book Show On Earth. When not typing, twirling about on stage, or being very dramatic on screen, Steven spends his time trying to spot thistlewumps at the bottom of the garden and catching dust pooks in jars. His *The Wrong Pong* series was shortlisted for the prestigious Roald Dahl Funny Prize.

www.stevenbutlerbooks.com

Steven L is an award-winning illustrator based in Brighton, not far from *The Nothing To See Here Hotel*! As well as designing all of the creatures you have just seen throughout this book, Steven also illustrates the *Shifty McGifty and Slippery Sam* series and Frank Cottrell Boyce's fiction titles. When he isn't drawing giant spiders and geriatric mermaids, Steven loves to eat ice cream on Brighton beach looking out for goblin pirate ships on the horizon.

www.stevenlenton.com

WELCOME TO

THE NOTHING to see HERE HOTEL

Have you read Frankie Banister's first blunkingly bonkers adventure?!